FIRE OF A DRAGON

Fallen Immortals 3

ALISA WOODS

Cover Design by Steven Novak

ISBN-13: 9781095744697

Fire of a Dragon (**Fallen Immortals 3**)
Paranormal Fairytale Romance

Lucian is a Dragon Prince of the House of Smoke... and he's dying. He has to spawn a dragonling to uphold the treaty that keeps the mortal world safe from the immortal Dark Fae, but a dragon's mate rarely survives the birth of a young dragon... and he can't face the horror of another woman's death on his hands. When he rescues a beautiful woman from a demon roaming the streets of Seattle, he has to seduce her without losing his heart... and before he turns into a feral dragon and breaks the treaty forever.

The *Fallen Immortals* series is a modern Beauty and the Beast story with flaming HOT dragon shifters, vengeful Dark Fae, and beguiling fallen angels.

Chapter One

ARABELLA'S SWEET BODY WAS SPLAYED OUT before him…

…and he was plunging into her once again.

Every thrust sparked literal magic between them, heightening their lovemaking. *Mated sex*. He'd never thought he would have it again, but here he was, cock-deep inside a woman who was carrying his child.

A woman he loved.

The thrill and chill of that rivaled the orgasm that was building deep in his loins. Arabella was on hands and knees, bent over on the sprawling couch in the great room of his lair, her whimpering-urgent sounds driving him on. It had been a week since the sealing, and they'd made love on nearly every square inch of his lair—floors, walls, tables, couches—anything with a surface they could stand, kneel or sit on... or prop up against. Sleeping and eating were the only things that punctuated the driving need to couple—on both their parts, now that Arabella bore his mark, the serpentine dragon tattoo that writhed with his magic as her back arched under the pounding of his cock. She was getting close—he was so intimately tuned to her body now, he could tell from the smallest quiver—and he knew she liked it hard right at the end, but he couldn't bring himself to pick up the pace. He knew the baby was safe inside her womb. He knew the lovemaking was one way to bathe the baby in a love-drenched magic environment that would just make him grow stronger and healthier. And he knew Arabella could take it now—the full strength of his lust, however strong he wanted it, now that she was sealed with his magic and made nearly as immortal as he was.

He just had an overwhelming urge to be gentle with her—to hold her and protect her and keep her from harm. Even the harm that came from carrying his child.

Although it was too late for that now.

Arabella banged back against him, driving him

deeper by shoving her delicious rear end up into his stroke. "God, Lucian! *Harder,*" she complained.

She probably thought he was teasing her.

He caressed her bottom, making her moan, but didn't put any more power into his thrust. "I don't want to hurt you, my treasure," he said softly. They were words straight from his heart, but he didn't know if she would take their meaning.

She groaned and gripped the back of the couch, leveraging back to bang into him again. Her beautiful green eyes blazed at him, half-lidded with the world's sexiest look thrown over her shoulder. "I don't care if you're an immortal dragon, Lucian Smoke," she ground out through her teeth. "I *will* find a way to hurt you if you keep teasing me like this."

He grinned, and like *that*, she lightened his heart. It was a magic she alone in the world possessed and just one of the many reasons she owned his heart.

"You shouldn't threaten a dragon, love." He bit his lip as he contemplated the best way to grant her wish. And bring her hard and fast to climax.

"That was no threat." She followed it up with a growl that was utterly sincere and made him almost laugh.

"Well, then," he said, barely holding in his humor, but pulling his cock from the delicious magic heat of her body. "I'd better do this right."

She muttered a cursing complaint as he left her body, but he quickly turned her and laid her on her back, ankles over his shoulders. She gasped as he took her hard, plunging even deeper with this position, plus gaining some sizzling hot friction—that magic spark wherever they touched—right on her swollen nub as he slammed into her body.

She shrieked with the first hard pound and arched her back. Her flesh quivered hot around him.

"You are *mine*, Arabella Sharp," he growled out as he slammed into her. He knew she loved it when he claimed her with his words and his body and his magic all at once. "And I *will* make you come."

"Oh God, yes. *Yes!*" She was folded up in half, a position they wouldn't be able to use for much longer, as the bump of the baby in her belly was already starting to show. Dragon gestation was accelerated and magical—like everything else *dragon* —and lasted only six weeks. At one week in, she was already showing the way a human pregnancy would halfway through the first trimester. A small rounding of her lovely belly. The barest sign of their love just beginning to manifest in the world. Lucian wanted so much just to hold and kiss her there, right at the soft rise that would become their son, but right now, in this moment, he was busy claiming her, deep and hard and fast.

Her shrieks grew, and she dug her fingers hard into his arms, which were holding him up and angling him just right to take her. When she came, it was a great shuddering release that squeezed down on him in waves. Between the hot pressure, her delicious cries, and the sparking magic between them, his own release rushed at him and seized hold of his body. He went rigid, sunk deep, and pumped more of his seed into her. It seemed to draw out forever, both of them riding the wave and barely holding on.

Holy magic, this woman.

As the wave passed, leaving a high buzz of post-climax pleasure behind, he released her legs and let them fall back to the couch. He stayed hovering over her, holding his weight with an elbow digging into the couch on either side. He was spent— emotionally and sexually—at least for the moment, with no desire to move or be anywhere else. He nuzzled the soft rounding of her belly, peppering it with gentle kisses. He knew all the lovemaking was his dragon nature's way of making sure the baby had the best chance. Like any dragonling, it was a magical creature carried by a human—a magic-enhanced human, to be sure, but the odds were still against everything going right. Any creature that arose from nothing more than the coupling of its parents was a small miracle, but creating an immortal was more than just a recombination of DNA between egg and sperm cells. Conditions in the mother had to be just right. And for a baby born into the House of Smoke, the requirements were even more extreme.

For a dragon prince, the mother's love had to be *True* for the sealing to take... and to remain sealed throughout the pregnancy. Arabella had survived the first burn of the sealing, so her love must have been True at that moment, and all the moments since. But there were another five weeks of magical transformation yet to go... and Lucian had given her every reason in the world to doubt him.

"Food." Arabella breathed the word a half second before the delightful tummy near Lucian's face rumbled its own protest. "I need food. Then probably more sex. But definitely food first." She picked up her head and peered down past the perky mounds of her breasts, still sitting at attention from their lovemaking. "You don't happen to have mint chocolate chip ice cream, do you?"

He smiled. "I could magic some for you, but it wouldn't be very filling."

She flopped back down on the couch and spoke to the ceiling two stories above. "Anything you've got, then. I could out-eat a linebacker for the Seahawks right now."

He growled, dropped a kiss on her belly, and rose from the couch. "No mentions of other men in my presence. Even theoretical men and theoretical food. No one is allowed to provide for you besides me." He gave her a playful scowl as he stepped away from the couch. Her eyes followed him, hungry for more than the food he was hurrying off to retrieve from the kitchen. Ordinarily, that look would stop him in his tracks and bring him back for more magical lovemaking, but *this*—this providing for her, literally bringing her food—was what he *really* wanted to do. It satisfied a deep and urgent need to give her real sustenance, not just pleasure, but something solid. It was trite, he knew that, but his happiness reached a near-giddy level as he rifled through the refrigerator and pantry for a bowl of grapes and some cheese and crackers. He sent a flutter of magic to his phone, texting his right-hand dragon, Cinaed, to pick up some mint chocolate chip ice cream ASAP, along with a host of other groceries. Lucian and Arabella hadn't left his lair in a week, and with groceries delivered to his door, they could stay in for the entire six-week pregnancy.

Which was exactly what Lucian had planned.

He quickly strode back to her, balancing the food on two hands. Arabella was still flopped out on the couch. He set the items down and bent to scoop her into his arms. Her hands automatically went to his chest, and his cock twitched at the touch. They were both completely naked and had spent most of the week that way—it had begun to feel normal along with the endless rounds of sex.

"Where are we going?" she asked, with a flicked look for the windows, one of her favored love-making spots. She liked it when he took her from behind, standing up, pressed against the glass and helpless against the onslaught while the beauty of the forest sprawled below.

But that wasn't what she needed right now.

"Nowhere." He curled up on the couch and nestled her into his lap.

Her eyes widened a bit from the sleepy haze the sex had brought over them. He lifted the chilled steel bowl of grapes and plucked one from the stem to feed to her. She took it and closed her eyes in appreciation as she bit into it.

"More," she said before it was even down.

He plucked another, but she just took the bowl and started devouring. He smiled and ate the grape himself. A dragon mate's appetite was legendary— the rapid gestation required an almost constant supply of food. Arabella stuffed several more grapes in her mouth, then cradled the bowl to her cheeks and moaned as the coolness of it seeped in.

He frowned. "Are you feeling hot?" A chill ran through his belly as if the cold metal bowl were pressed there. She had survived the first burn of the sealing, but there were so many other points in the gestation that could go wrong... and one of the possible symptoms was a fever. A raging magical fever that couldn't be stopped and would eventually burn her to ash.

"Well, yeah," she said, like that should be obvious. "Your Olympic gymnast style sex did heat me up just a little." She gave him a sly smirk.

He tried to keep his sigh of relief inside. "You have to tell me if it's too much... if it's more than you can..." His gaze dropped to her belly, softly rounded, which was serving as a table for the grape bowl now.

"Lucian, *I'm fine.*"

He had been asking that very thing a lot throughout the week. So many ways to die... and only one narrow pathway to surviving. But it was no help to tell her, to worry her... the stress alone could do it. He held in the other concerns that were crowding to get out, but that he couldn't give voice to. Worrying might also bring out her doubts about *him*—the ones she had every right to have. And he couldn't risk that.

"Is that cheese?" She was peering past her bare knees to the triangle of Cantal and sleeve of crackers on the couch.

He picked up the cheese, shifted one finger into a talon, and sliced open the packaging.

"That's handy," she said with a small, teasing smile.

"All the better to feed my lady love." He gave her a play-scowl, then sliced a chunk of the cheese, married it with a cracker, and fed it to her.

"Oh man, that's good," she said around a mouthful.

"It's aged from the South of France." His native stomping grounds had been left behind long ago, but his taste for some of the finer foods had never disappeared.

She patted her belly and swallowed before speaking. "Baby approves of fancy cheese food. Wants more."

He smiled wide and sliced her another chunk. He kept feeding her, and they stayed quiet a moment, skin to skin, primal and wrapped in love. His joy in it would have been complete except for the shadow of fear looming over. He steeled his expression to keep it from showing on his face and just focused on slowly stroking the sealing mark on her back—something he knew kept a steady thrum of pleasure pulsing through her body—and feeding her more when she was ready.

When she had gulped down half the cheese and all of the grapes, she paused for a moment between bites. And peered at him.

He was being too quiet.

"Tell me more about being immortal," she said conversationally, but there was a sharpness in her eyes. She was probing for something. "No holding back. I'm sealed now, so just give it to me straight."

"Well, you're not invincible," he said, trying to keep the tightness out of his voice. "But you *are* literally bullet proof."

She held out her hand, palm up. "So I could stop a bullet with my bare hand?"

He placed a slice of cheese in it. "I wouldn't recommend testing that out," he said with a scowl. "The bullet won't penetrate your skin, but a big enough force could take your hand right off."

"So my skin's tough." She popped the cheese in her mouth then examined her hand like she didn't quite believe him.

He took it and kissed it. "Your hand is lovely and soft and sexy as hell when it's on my body."

Her eyes glittered, and he'd happily go for more sex rather than have this discussion.

But she pulled her hand back and pressed on. "So the only thing that can cut me is dragon claws?" She peered intently at him.

He fought against the visions that dredged up. *Cara drenched in blood.* His own talons dipped in it. The sounds when she died trying to give life to their son... he pushed those thoughts away. "Dragon talons and angel blades and a few other kinds of magic you don't need to worry about."

"Because you're going to keep me safe." And she said it with such certainty that relief gushed through him.

"I'm not leaving your side, Arabella. Not for a moment." Of that much, he was certain. If only it were just external dangers that she faced.

She nodded like this was a given. "What else?"

He furrowed his brow, wondering what she was after. "You should now have a host of other dragon-like qualities. You'll have a dragon-sized passion for sex."

She smirked. "I noticed that."

He lifted the reddish-tinted brown hair that had fallen forward to conceal one of her breasts. Along the way, he trailed his finger across her skin, and it sparked pleasure. Her eyes half-lidded. "And that sex will be magic enhanced."

"Noticed that, too," she breathed, her voice dropping.

He leaned in to kiss her neck and whisper in her ear. "You'll have enhanced smell. More sensitive touch. Keener vision." He pulled back and peered into her eyes. "You'll be able to see through glamour. No immortal will be able to trick your eyes with their magic."

The incipient lust dropped from her face. "Like Zephan."

"Like Zephan." The bastard fae prince of the Winter Court had tried to seduce her by wearing a glamour of Lucian's skin. But his Arabella hadn't been fooled, even without the help of seeing through the fae's glamour. "But he's not going to bother us anyway. He's magically sworn not to hurt you, which is stronger even than the treaty. That kind of magic is *binding*. He literally *can't* touch you or hurt you in any way."

But Arabella was frowning now.

"I promise, you have nothing to fear from the outside world now, my love." He studied her face. "Please don't hold back, Arabella. If you have anything you want to say… any feelings that aren't quite right…" *Any doubts you have about me…* but he couldn't say that. "You *must* tell me, my love."

Her hand went to her belly, cradling it and their son inside, but she just stared at some indefinable spot on the couch, avoiding his gaze. He held his breath, waiting.

Slowly, she brought her gaze up to meet his. Her blazing green eyes were so intense, it felt like they were piercing his soul. "I will *never* doubt my love for you, Lucian."

Emotion welled up and threatened to choke him. Because he knew that vow was useless—True Love couldn't be forced or promised. It could only be *True*. And it could be shattered in an instant by any number of doubts for which he had already planted the seeds with no way to root them out.

He couldn't let any of that show because, above

all things, right now and for the next five weeks, he needed to be the kind of man she *could* love. He cupped a hand to her cheek, fighting through the lump in his throat to speak. "I would do anything for you, Arabella Sharp. You and our son. You are everything to me." It was true, and it was necessary, and he prayed to all that was magic that she could hear the truth of those words.

"Prove it," she said, sending a flutter of panic icing through his heart. But then she turned in his lap so that she was suddenly straddling his legs. Her hand left her belly and found his cock, grasping it and giving it a good, hard stroke. It instantly came to life, growing hard in her grip. "Show me just how much you love me," she whispered, stroking him harder and pressing her chest to his face.

He simply growled in return and grasped hold of her hips, pulling her in and down, impaling her on his already rock-hard erection. She gasped and started riding him, sparking pleasure with every bounce. Her head tipped back, and the gasps coming from her were so pleasure-filled, he wondered if she were coming already.

He let her ride, glad to be free of the dangerous zone where she might wonder about his love or the dangers ahead or the insanity that she'd signed up for—*carrying his dragonling.*

Sex and food. Food and sex. He could do this, keep her going, keep her alive.

Five more weeks…

Chapter Two

AFTER ALMOST TWO WEEKS OF BEING NAKED, IT FELT strange for Arabella to have clothes on.

Lucian was by her side, per usual, as they walked down the corridor toward the guest apartment that used to be her home—her temporary home, at least. They had spent so much time intertwined, intimately locked, having endless rounds of sex, but now that they were outside his lair, Lucian seemed to want to be even closer. His arm was draped protectively around her. Their steps were in sync. He didn't seem to realize that a little personal space was in order, especially if they were going to be around other people.

"I have to see Rachel *alone,*" Arabella said as

they rounded a corner and approached the door to the guest apartment.

"I'm not going to leave your side," Lucian said, tightly. His hand squeezed her shoulder for emphasis. "I already told you that. And besides we shouldn't even be outside the lair—you're barely two weeks into the pregnancy. We should be at home."

Arabella knew he was stressed, but they couldn't stay in the lair forever. And there was a lingering unspoken topic—Cara's death during her pregnancy, at Lucian's hands as he tried to save their unborn son—that hung between them, making it worse. But she *wasn't* Cara. Lucian's previous mate had been seduced by Zephan, the fae Prince. Arabella doubted Lucian knew that, but she could too easily imagine how it had just wrecked the woman. It must have caused Cara to doubt her love for Lucian, and that was what spelled her doom. But that *wasn't* going to happen to Arabella. And Lucian needed to back off and let her take care of things with her best friend. Rachel had to be going crazy not having heard from Arabella for almost two weeks—even if her best friend knew she was in the keep, locked up with a gorgeous dragon shifter, having amazing sex.

Arabella wriggled out from under Lucian's hold.

He let her go with a look that was glowering.

"I have to talk to Rachel alone," Arabella ground out between her teeth. She couldn't believe he couldn't just *get* this. "She's going to be so angry at me—I need time alone to smooth it over."

"She has no cause for anger." Lucian wasn't conceding this one bit.

"You don't know Rachel—she doesn't need a cause." Arabella stopped in front of the door but didn't knock. "Besides, she *does* have cause." She couldn't believe he was forcing her to say this, but she would, if she had to.

"She was worried you wouldn't survive the sealing," he said, the tension ramping up in his voice. "But you did. Why would she still be angry?"

"Because I might yet die."

Lucian's face dropped to blankness, and he just blinked. But he didn't have any immediate comeback.

Arabella pounded on the door.

It opened immediately, but the person on the other side of the door wasn't Rachel—it was Cinaed, Lucian's right-hand dragon. The tall, muscular, reddish-haired dragon shifter was hot for Rachel, and Arabella had left him alone with her for two weeks with explicit permission to take her best friend to bed. If they wanted to. Arabella didn't know if that had happened, but if Cinaed took Lucian's side and tried to keep Arabella from having a one-on-one girl discussion with her best friend, she would lay them both out.

"Thank magic you're here," Cinaed said, gesturing her inside.

Arabella brushed past him. "Where is she?" She scanned the great room that was off the entranceway, but it was empty.

Lucian closed the door behind them.

Cinaed hovered close, looking Arabella over like he wanted to hug her, or something, but didn't quite have the bravery to do it. His gaze kept bouncing down to her belly and back up to her eyes as if he expected her to be incapacitated by the tiny bump that was her son.

His gaze finally settled on her eyes. "She's hiding in the bedroom. Claims she doesn't want to speak to you, my lady, but it's a lie. She does."

Arabella put a hand on Cinaed's shoulder, and her touch seemed to make him relax. "I know." Then she glanced at Lucian, whose scowl was just getting darker. "I'm going in. You stay here."

She turned her back on Lucian and marched

towards the bedroom in the back of the apartment. But Lucian wasn't letting this go—he was right at her heels, and he caught her elbow before she reached the door.

Arabella stopped and dropped her voice, not wanting Rachel to hear them, even through the door. "Lucian Smoke, I swear to God—"

But his arms simply went around her, and he pulled her into his chest. His touch always disarmed her—*man, he was playing dirty.*

Then he whispered into her hair, "Take čare of your friend. But all the demons in hell couldn't pull me from this door. I'll be waiting for you."

He released her.

She rolled her eyes. "It's not like I'm going through the gates of the underworld here." She shook her head, but his slightly terrified look wrenched the sympathy out of her. "Oh, for God's sake." She leaned up and gave him a quick kiss on the cheek, then turned away and wrenched open the bedroom door, quickly scuttling in and closing it behind her.

Rachel was standing at the window, her back turned to Arabella. But she could tell by the stiffness of her best friend's stance that she was well-aware of Arabella.

"Cinaed explained it to me," Rachel said. Arabella had never heard so much anger in her voice. "Either you're going to die giving birth to this *thing*… or you're going to live forever as Lucian's baby mama. Either way, I'm fucked."

Okay, *that* pissed her off. "If I live, it won't be forever—just for five hundred years. And that *thing* is my son."

The anger in Arabella's voice must have gotten through the thick wall she knew Rachel liked to throw up against anything that might hurt her heart. Arabella had never been on the other side of that wall—she'd seen it put up time and again, against everything and everyone else in the world, but not her. Never her.

Rachel turned to her with wide eyes, her shoulders dropping. "Your son?" There were tears in her eyes.

"I can already feel the baby, Rach. Sweet and beautiful and made of magic. And I already love him." There was a catch in her voice, and Rachel's tears let loose. Arabella hadn't seen her cry since… well, she couldn't remember *ever* seeing Rachel cry. Not out of sadness or love—occasionally out of anger or fear. Arabella hurried across the room and threw her arms around Rachel's neck.

She latched on like she was drowning. "It's not fair!" she sobbed into Arabella's hair. "I lose you either way."

"No, it's *me* who loses *you.*" Arabella squeezed her tighter, and she could feel Rachel relax, just a little. "You're staying with me through this—I need you, Rach. I need your support. And God, I *so* need a place to come that's not Lucian's lair because I'm going nuts in there."

Rachel sniffed and pulled back, grasping hold of Arabella's shoulders and staring her in the eyes. "Is that damn dragon shifter keeping you prisoner? I swear to God, I will kick his ass—"

A crazy laugh erupted deep inside Arabella. "He's right outside the door if that tells you anything. And I'm sure he can hear every word we're saying."

Rachel wrenched her head toward the door and threw her words at it. "Fuck you, Lucian Smoke! Fuck you for knocking up my best friend!"

Now the giggles were seriously getting hold of Arabella. She fought them down.

Rachel turned a mournful look back to her. "Well, *of course,* you have me for support during this whole…" She gestured to Arabella's body. "… dragon pregnancy thing. But you're not going to want me around after that. There's no place for me here."

Arabella's humor died completely. "Yes, there is. You and I—we're sisters. We stick together, remember?"

Rachel's face pinched up again, and it looked like the tears were coming back. "You're mated now. And if you don't die from this whole crazy-ass thing, you'll be too busy raising the baby."

"I better not be! Who do you think is going to run the business?" Arabella gave her an incredulous look. "What about all the women we help? All the ones who need us to save them from the assholes in their life? I'm not going to give that up, Rach. I've work too hard for it." She gave her best friend a stern look. "Don't you go wimping out on me. I'm having this baby, and I'm going to take care of him, but our work is too important to let fall by the wayside. The only way to make that happen is with *your* help. Are you with me?"

Rachel scowled at her. "How is that even a question?"

Arabella nodded. "That's more like it." She glanced at the door. "Besides, staying here might not be too bad. What about Cinaed?"

Rachel's scowl got darker. "What about him?"

"Have you slept with him yet?" She arched her eyebrows.

Rachel drew back, her expression filled with disgust. "That *dragon?* No. What are you even talking about?"

Arabella found herself rolling her eyes for the second time in as many minutes. Why did the people she loved have to be so stubbornly obtuse? "Oh, come on! He's super hot, and I've seen the way he looks at you. I know he wants to do you, Rachel."

"Well, of course, he does!" She looked offended. "What's not to love here?" She gestured to her ample chest and curvy figure. The truth was that Arabella's best friend was super hot herself—one reason why she always had drop-dead gorgeous guys after her. That wasn't the problem. It was that Rachel had been burned pretty much every single time. And not by dragonfire... just the regular human-asshole-type burn.

Rachel scowled. "Cinaed is hot and nice and, yes, I can tell he wants me bad—and yet he hasn't made even the slightest move. What the hell am I supposed to do with that?" She threw an accusing finger toward the door. "If he just wanted to fuck, I could do that. But he doesn't. It's like... like he's holding out for something more. And you *know* I can't do that. I am *not* making that mistake again. He's playing some kind of head game. They *all* play games, but the ones who are hotter than sin are especially good at it. And I'm no fool."

Arabella frowned. "Cinaed's not like that. You know that."

"Why?" Her voice dripped with ice. "Because he's a sexy dragon shifter? That just makes him hotter… in all the different meanings of that word. But he's still a man, Arabella."

"So all this time in the apartment together, you guys haven't…?" She was frankly amazed Rachel hadn't just gone for one really hot night and then dumped Cinaed. Because that was her *modus operandi*. Maybe it was because she knew she couldn't just shove him out the door when she was done with him.

The disgust was back on Rachel's face. "No. And I'm not going to. End of story."

Arabella sighed. "Okay, fine. But I'm just saying… you heard him talk about his family, just like I did, Rach."

"So what? So he lost his family. That's happened to lots of people." Rachel's eyes turned hard now, and Arabella understood where she was coming from. Both of them had been through the foster system together because they had lost their families early on. It had been hard and awful, and no one in the system had ever loved them, not truly —except each other. It was why they were sisters. To know Cinaed had the same thing happen to him, only more violently, having his parents torn from him... and yet, he still believed in love... well, Arabella could see how that would rankle. Pretty bad.

"Maybe you two can be friends," she said.

"Yeah, okay." Rachel folded her arms. "Maybe."

Arabella smiled and slid one arm around her best friend's shoulders, squeezing tight. "Holy shit, I've missed you."

"Hey, I'm not the one off fucking her brains out with some hot guy instead of hanging out with, you know, her best friend on the planet." But there was no heat behind it, and Rachel's arm slipped around her waist and squeezed back.

Arabella released her. "We better get back out there before Lucian loses his mind."

Rachel squinted at her. "What is it with these fucking dragons? So damn overprotective."

Arabella gestured her toward the door. "Well,

it's not as if there aren't a few dangerous things out in the world. But I know Lucian's going to protect me from them. It's kind of his job now to proactively worry overtime."

Rachel shrugged as they reached the door. Arabella pulled it open, and sure enough, Lucian was lurking outside. Cinaed had a hand on his shoulder, gripping tight as if he was physically restraining Lucian from breaking through and coming after her.

Arabella just shook her head, but before she could say anything, Cinaed hustled past Rachel and motioned Arabella back into the bedroom.

"A word with you, my lady," he said as he quickly closed the door, leaving a gap-mouthed Lucian still outside.

The two of them were alone in the room. Arabella frowned. "What's up?"

Cinaed dropped to one knee, head bent, arms splayed out to the side in some kind of bizarre dramatic bowing thing. He spoke loudly with this odd, formal tone in his lilting Irish accent. "Your love for my lord is True, my lady, and I pledge my life to protect yours and the future prince of the House of Smoke."

She grinned. "Okay." It was kind of adorable, she had to admit.

Cinaed looked up, his eyes shining but serious. "You should know, my lady, that my prince loves you more than anything else on this earth. It's the kind of love a dragon such as myself can only wish for some day. Please tell me you understand this."

She was back to frowning again. "Yes, I understand that."

Relief washed over Cinaed's face, and he climbed to his feet. His expression was less formal, but no less serious now. "I wanted to speak to you privately, my lady, about a personal matter…" He glanced at the door. "One we have discussed previously."

Recognition dawned in Arabella's mind. "This is about Rachel."

He nodded and looked adorably bashful, dropping his gaze and biting his lip. He worried it for a moment, then looked back up. "I know that you gave me leave to pursue her—although I am not quite sure she wishes to be pursued—but I have been holding back."

"Oh?" Arabella bit back the words that she wanted to say, giving him a chance to have his say.

But she was pretty sure Rachel *did* want to be pursued, no matter what she claimed.

"My lady is at a critical time in carrying the young future prince. I wish to do nothing that would give you even a moment's pause or worry. So I will respect your prior wishes and stay away from your lady in waiting. But after the baby is born... I may approach her. If I were to... approach her... do you think she would be receptive to it?"

"Cinaed, just ask her. Or better yet, kiss her. It's really all right."

Cinaed scowled. "I am familiar with how to seduce a woman, my lady."

Arabella nearly laughed, but she figured that probably wasn't such a good idea.

"It is not *bedding* your maid that worries me. It's whether she's capable of being more than a bedmate. Of those, I've had plenty. That's not what I'm looking for."

Arabella bit her lip. That was a bit trickier.

"You should know," Cinaed rushed out, "that mating with an ordinary dragon is not so treacherous as with a prince of the House of Smoke. Rachel's love would *not* have to be True in order to survive the sealing. There are many vile dragons who force themselves on their chosen mates and still manage to produce dragonlings." Then he stopped as if he knew what he wanted to say, but he was hesitating to give it voice.

"But that's not what you want, right?" Arabella asked. "You want True Love as well."

His voice dropped. "I knew my lady would understand."

Arabella grimaced, and the small hairs on the back of her neck rose. Because what did she know about love, really? And Rachel knew even less. The two of them loved each other like sisters—but neither one had ever truly loved a man. Not until Lucian came along. Arabella thought she had before, but that had been a mistake. She supposed there was no objective proof of Lucian's love for her, but there was no real doubt in her mind. Any fool could see the man lived for her. But for Rachel... "Cinaed, you have to know I want that— I want Rachel to have what I have with Lucian. I just don't know if... well, if she can. She just really doesn't trust guys at all. I told her you're different, but... I don't know. I'm sorry, does that help at all?"

"Yes, my lady," he said, dipping his head, looking disappointed. He turned to leave, but she caught him by the shoulder and then threw her arms around his neck to hug him.

He seemed startled, but he lightly patted her back in return.

"It's all going to work out, Cinaed. I promise," she whispered then released him.

He gave her a sharp nod and turned to the door to open it.

Lucian was hovering literally in the doorway. It was annoying and adorable at the same time, and she fervently hoped that Cinaed and Rachel could figure out a way to have this thing she had with Lucian. She may not really understand love, but she knew it when she saw it in Lucian's eyes. And felt it in her own heart.

"Okay, caveman," Arabella said with a grin. "You can haul me back to your lair now and have your way with me."

The way Lucian's eyes lit up sent a shiver of excitement through her. Carrying a dragonling for a prince of the House of Smoke might yet kill her... but she'd be damned if the ride wasn't worth the price of admission.

Chapter Three

Arabella had reached the end of her second week, and Lucian couldn't be more relieved.

Traditionally, the most dangerous times were the sealing, the first fortnight, and then the birth of the dragonling. In that order. Arabella had survived the first two danger points, and now the true recognition of the dragonling's presence could be made. Formality would ensue. They were expected to come out of seclusion, but Lucian would still rather keep Arabella safely squirreled away with him alone.

He'd struck a compromise with his brothers, given the unique circumstances of the pregnancy, to bring some of the formal proceedings to his lair. The problem, in truth, wasn't his brothers—it was his mother, the queen. After not too long, she would insist that they make a public appearance. But for now, he and Arabella could remain in the lair, albeit with clothes on and receiving guests. It was an unsettling change of pace after a rather satisfying two days of him providing pleasure and food for her nearly around the clock.

Arabella stood in front of the bedroom mirror, looking stunning in the white-and-gold brocaded dress he had conjured for her. It was a fashionable style from the days of his upbringing in France—five hundred years out of date, but somehow that made it suitably old-fashioned and fittingly formal for the occasion.

Arabella tugged at the tight fit of the bodice over her growing belly. "Are you sure this is how it's supposed to fit?"

He came up from behind her and slid his hands around to cup the small rise. "Stop complaining, or I will need to take it off you one more time before our guests arrive."

She scowled, then she shoved his hands away and straightened her shoulders. "I know I'm tremendously irresistible," she said with one arched eyebrow that truly made him want to disrobe her immediately. "But this baby doesn't just belong to us, does it? It belongs to your family as well."

"Truer words have rarely been spoken." He gave her a smirk. "They'll have gifts, you know. I hope you'll accept them."

She gave him a look like he was slightly crazed. "Why wouldn't I?"

He grimaced slightly. "Well, I have no idea what the gifts may be, but I imagine they're not your traditional baby shower items."

"Well, this is not your traditional baby." She lifted her chin and seemed proud of that fact. Yet another reason for him to love her. "It's not like I've ever been to a baby shower anyway. I'll hardly know the difference."

He cupped her cheeks in his hands and kissed her softly. "Stop making me want you, woman."

"You don't mean that at all, Lucian Smoke," she taunted, daring him with her eyes.

He growled and gave her a swat on the bottom, lightly, but enough to draw small shriek out of her. She beat on his shoulder with a fist, then he caught it and drew her back against the door of the bedroom. He went in to kiss her, but she turned her head.

"Lucian! Stop it!" She was laughing, and truthfully, it was difficult for him to pull back.

But a sound at the door downstairs beckoned them.

He sighed and released her. "I fervently hope my brothers don't plan to stay long." And he meant every word of that.

He escorted her downstairs, and the two of them went to the door together to greet their guests. When he magicked open the door, it was only Leksander and Erelah. Leonidas had apparently decided not to be on time, which didn't terribly surprise Lucian, but he hoped that would mean his visit would be brief when it happened. And it would give Lucian an excuse to kick him out sooner.

"Leksander. Erelah. May I introduce my mate, Arabella," Lucian said with a properly official tone. Leksander had met Arabella before, but Lucian was surprised to see Erelah at his door. He gave a quick frowning and questioning look to his brother, who just shook his head.

Erelah gasped as she took in Arabella's gown. "You are a vision!" she cried. The angeling moved quickly forward to embrace Arabella. "Oh, you are a wonder! A true beauty!"

Leksander stood behind her, looking awkward.

Lucian grimaced.

Angels had a love for humans that bordered on unseemly. That was how half-human, half-angel beings like Erelah were made after all. Although the resulting product—angelings—seemed more unearthly to Lucian than human-like.

For her part, Arabella seemed startled, but accepting. She managed to get her arms around Erelah just as she was pulling back, adding even more awkwardness. The only person who seemed not to sense the strangeness of this gushing love was Erelah herself. Like their angel fathers, angelings' love for humans knew no bounds—their understanding of etiquette and human social norms was a little more stunted.

Erelah clasped her hands together, joy lighting up her face.

"Please come in." Lucian invited them with a sweep of his arm. Erelah hooked her arm around Arabella's and dragged her towards the great room. Arabella had a smile on her face, Erelah's enthusiasm clearly infectious. Lucian watched them go and waited for his brother to step in.

Leksander tipped his head toward Lucian and dropped his voice. "She insisted on coming. I'm sorry."

"Worry not, my brother," Lucian said with a smile. "I'm sure she means well enough."

"You know she effusively loves any human," Leksander said, still keeping his voice hushed as they walked towards the great room where the two women had already found a spot by the windows together. "But when she heard Arabella was with child, she just about lost her damn mind."

"Because the baby fulfills the treaty?" Lucian asked. "Or is there some other angel strangeness I should be aware of?" Angelings were almost as unfathomable as the fae—even though they were immortal enemies, they shared a certain inscrutability. The angelings at least had a fundamentally good nature, even though their true angel parentage was mixed with human failings as well as DNA. Their strangeness made Lucian wonder why Leksander was so drawn to Erelah's kind, but one look at the beautiful angeling, and it was easy to see why he had lost his heart to her. Long, ethereally blonde hair. Thin, elegant arms and legs that went on forever. Erelah was more beautiful than any human, a divine beauty visited upon her by her father's angel nature. She was obtuse to it as well, along with its effect on his brother. But once smitten,

Lucian doubted Leksander, or any man, could ever love a mere human again.

Leksander's gaze was already trained on her. "I'm fairly certain her enthusiasm is simply because your son will be the next prince of the House of Smoke, protector of humanity, fulfiller of the treaty, and all around fantastic guy." He smiled. "If there's one thing an angeling likes more than humans, it's someone who can save *all* of humanity." He looked chagrined at this.

Perhaps if his brother were the crown prince— if he had been born before Lucian and fate had delivered him to that role—he could win his angeling's love after all. Although Lucian wondered if an angel was even capable of something like the True Love that humans and dragons could share.

He clapped a hand on his brother's shoulder and gave it a squeeze. "Perhaps her love for the baby prince will give her cause to come around the keep more often."

Leksander's smile was almost pained. "One can hope."

Lucian felt the sadness of it like a strike on his heart. They approached the two women standing by the two-story window. Erelah still hadn't let go of

Arabella's hands, clasping them and gazing in wonder at her face.

"You among all women are blessed, Arabella Sharp," Erelah gushed.

"Um… yeah. Suppose that's true." Arabella's sprinkling of freckles became more pronounced under her embarrassment.

Lucian wanted to interject something, but Erelah wasn't finished. "Your son will save the world!" She grasped harder onto Arabella's hands. "That does not happen very often." She gave Arabella a wink.

Leksander looked stricken. Lucian just shook his head.

Then Erelah dropped to one knee in front of Arabella. His mate frowned, and even Lucian was wondering what in the world Erelah was doing. She swept her hands wide then brought them close to hover over Arabella's belly. She was staring intently as if she could peer inside the womb. For a flash instant, Lucian wondered if she actually could. His own fae senses could taste the small beginnings of the child that was inside Arabella's belly. He'd already fallen in love with his own son, already knew him in a way that he wondered if even Arabella did. Full of new life. Bursting with innocence. It was said that unborn children were closer to heaven than even True Angels because of the newness of their being. And this being was half human, so perhaps Erelah, who was half angel, could reach his son in a way that others might not. Either way, an awkward, breath-held moment slowly passed.

Then Erelah asked Arabella, "May I give him a kiss?"

What? Lucian threw a look to Leksander, who was fighting a smile. His brother gave him a short nod, reassuring him, but Lucian still wasn't quite sure what the angeling meant.

"Um... I guess." Arabella was looking to him for reassurance as well.

Lucian gave her a nod. Reluctantly.

Erelah took hold of Arabella's hips and drew her belly closer to her lips. Lucian wasn't alarmed, but it was one of the stranger things he'd seen an angeling do.

Arabella's face contorted. "Oh, um, okay..."

But Erelah wasn't paying attention—she was entirely focused on Arabella's belly. A fierce look crossed her face, a kind of rapturous, intense love. Then she closed the final gap and pressed an open mouth kiss to the white brocaded cloth that covered

Arabella's skin. Erelah exhaled low and deep, and Lucian finally realized what she was doing.

Giving his son a life kiss.

Tears pricked the back of Lucian's eyes, and emotion suddenly choked him. It was a divine kiss, a life-giving kiss, the breathing of life energy into his unborn son, strengthening him with a magic even more powerful than the dragon and fae magic that were mixed in the patronage of his House of Smoke bloodline.

"Oh! *Wow,*" Arabella breathed. There was awe in her voice, and Lucian could only imagine how it must feel to be on the receiving end of an angel kiss. Erelah, for all her awkwardness, gained an esteem in Lucian's eyes that would never be diminished— she was bestowing a blessing, a very real and tangible blessing, that might enable his son to live through the difficult pregnancy and birth ahead.

It took three long seconds, but Erelah finally finished and rose up again, her face flushed with the glory of bestowing her gift. It reminded Lucian of when she brought the demon-infected human back to life in the alley—that same fervent, almost sexual rush of pleasure that seemed to set her face alight. Angelings were generally very chaste, but some of their stranged acts seemed rife with the kind of pleasure Lucian normally associated with the bedroom.

"Thank you, angeling," Lucian managed to get out past the lump in his throat.

Erelah beamed, her face radiating joy. "I have yet another gift, but this one is for your mate."

Lucian nodded his permission, not that she needed it. He was still overcome with what she had just done. But when she whipped out an angel blade and held it up high, panic surged through him. Before he could choke out words or even move, Erelah turned the blade around and held it out handle-first to Arabella.

She was equally stunned and just stared at the blade for a moment.

Lucian cursed under his breath and glared at Leksander. His brother's eyes were squeezed shut momentarily. He opened them and wordlessly gave Lucian an apology for his angeling brandishing the one thing besides dragon talons that could pierce Arabella's skin and take the life of both her and his dragonling.

"It's beautiful," Arabella said, tentative, and still staring at the blade without taking it. "Are you sure you want to part with it?"

"I've fashioned this one especially for you,"

Erelah gushed. "It has been imbued with a blessing just for you and your child. It's meant to protect you and him throughout both of your very long lives and bring you many blessings."

The tension seemed to go out of Arabella's body. She took the blade and held it up. It truly was beautiful, like everything made from angel magic. It glinted in the early morning sun, its white blade glowing with pure angel energy and the carved handle gleaming ebony.

"Thank you." Arabella gave her a slight bow. "It's the perfect gift. Both of them." She leaned forward and embraced the angeling, a move that seemed to light Erelah up from within. A humming sound, high in pitch and booming in nature welled up from somewhere inside the angeling's body. It was only an echo of an angel-song, but the power of it vibrated through Lucian's body. Leksander was struck by it, too, given the way his eyes filled with longing and desire. Even Arabella seemed struck by it, and their hug went on and on.

Lucian was ready to break it up when the door toned.

"That must be Leonidas," Lucian said.

Leksander was transfixed by his angeling.

Arabella and Erelah were still locked in their embrace.

"I guess I'll go let him in." Lucian just shook his head and went to the door.

Once it opened, Leonidas asked without preamble, "Where is our princess?"

Lucian gestured him in. "Receiving her gifts from the angeling."

"Nothing horrifying, I hope?" He strode inside, peering down the entranceway toward the great room, looking for Arabella.

"Only slightly," Lucian said. "Thank you for coming." He managed to keep most of the sarcasm out of his voice, given that Leonidas was only a few minutes past the appointed time.

"I had trouble selecting the proper gift," he said tightly, striding into the great room.

Lucian caught up to him just as Leksander and Erelah were turning to leave.

Leksander gave Leonidas a nod of hello, which Leonidas barely acknowledged, his gaze already locked on Arabella. Lucian didn't like the intense look on his face. Erelah was still floating on her high of interaction with Lucian's mate and unborn son. The giddy look on her face was carrying her toward the front door without noticing the fact that

Leonidas was even in the room. Leonidas broke away from them and headed towards Arabella.

Lucian was about to go after him, but Leksander caught his arm and said quietly, "I figured it was time for us to leave." He flicked a look at Erelah floating toward the door on light angel steps. Her angelsong had shifted to a frequency so high that most humans wouldn't be able to hear it.

"Thank you, my brother." He looked to the angeling. "And to Erelah. Thanks doesn't seem… enough."

Leksander nodded and straggled after her.

Lucian turned back to find Leonidas already holding Arabella's hands while talking quietly to her next to the window. Lucian was struck by a strange jealousy—he knew his brother would never threaten his treasure in any way, but the primal part of him that wanted to protect her from anything and everything still surged at the sight of another man's hands on her.

He strode over to the window to join them.

Leonidas dropped her hands and stepped back as Lucian approached, his head deferentially dipping to acknowledge Lucian's primacy in the situation. Just for extra measure, Lucian slid his arm around Arabella's waist, claiming her with his touch.

Leonidas's smile was genuine but sad. Lucian felt a strike of shame for his possessiveness, given the curse that his brother carried that would never allow him the same pleasure Lucian had with Arabella.

"Leonidas was just telling me how happy he was for us," Arabella said, her gaze flicking between the two of them. She seemed to sense the tension.

Lucian tipped his head to his brother, his grimace hopefully seen for the apology it was. "Uncle Leonidas does have a certain ring to it."

His brother sprouted a smile, then averted his gaze out the window. Lucian just prayed to all the forces of the universe that Leonidas would actually be able to claim that title.

Then he looked back to them and smirked. "I'll be the debauched uncle that teaches him how to drink hearty and chase women." He gave a mock look of shock to Arabella. "I'll wait until he's of age, of course."

Arabella was stifling a laugh behind her hand.

Leonidas's humor fled, and a serious expression took its place. "It is fortunate that this child will not be female because I am sure to love it, and that might spell disaster for me personally."

The humor dropped away from Arabella's face as well.

Lucian doubted she really understood the full measure of what Leonidas meant. "She's our princess now, Leonidas," Lucian said, gently. "She should know the truth of your situation."

"Yes, I suppose." Still, his brother seemed to hesitate.

"If you do not wish it…" Lucian was doubly a fool for bringing it up. It was bad enough that he flaunted his own love in the face of his brother's tragedy. He really didn't need to poke at old wounds as well.

Leonidas held up a hand to wave him off. "No, it is after all four-hundred-year-old news."

"Is this about your curse?" Arabella asked, her eyes keen upon Leonidas.

He gave her a bemused smile. "Yes. My curse." He drew in a breath and let it out slow. "Once upon a time, there was a witch who loved me. Sadly, I was a young and stupid dragon, hardly ready to settle down but very enthusiastic in bed." He was scowling as he said it, but then he lifted both eyebrows and smirked at Arabella. "My princess, now that you are a mated woman, you might understand my fascination with sex with a witch. I'm told it's much like mated sex in its rather... *enhanced* features."

Arabella's eyebrows lifted as well. "Oh. It's the..." She gestured between herself and Lucian. "It's like that?"

Leonidas nodded. "Oh yes. It's like *that.*" He shook his head, becoming serious once more. "Unfortunately, I experienced all of that way too young in my somewhat doomed dragon lifetime. And in my youthful stupidity, I failed to see that this young woman, this young witch..." He went back to staring out the window for a moment and seemed to be mustering words.

Lucian felt a stab for his brother's loss. And what he would never gain.

Leonidas cleared his throat. "Well, let's just say that she deserved better than me. And she was well aware of that fact." He looked back to Arabella. "She put a curse on me such that I will never be able to love another woman. If I do, I'll turn wyvern, just as Lucian was threatening to do before you saved him, my dear princess, from that fate. You and my little nephew." He dropped his gaze to

Arabella's belly. He reached out a hand and gently held it to her womb.

Emotion surged through Lucian again as the runes on Leonidas's arm scurried down to his hand. He was bringing his healing magic to bear on the child.

"*Forserum transpara thas sharon et sutta es. En domini et domini et domini.*" It was dragontongue. With a little bit of fae thrown in. An ancient spell. A healing spell. A protective spell. Leonidas lifted his hand free and smiled at Arabella.

"I don't have much to give you that you don't already possess. This small protective spell might ease this young dragonling into the world. That is my hope, at least." Leonidas's eyes glittered with what Lucian feared might be tears.

He turned to face Lucian. "My brother, you have found a treasure indeed. My happiness for the two of you knows no bounds. You and your princess and your beautiful son will live long past me. I hope you will understand if I spoil him mercilessly in the time I have left."

Arabella looked stricken, but Lucian was compelled to pull his brother into a fierce hug. "He will be as your son as well," Lucian choked out.

Then he roughly shoved his brother away as the

two of them worked to get their raging emotions under control. The struggle was made infinitely harder when Lucian saw Arabella's face streaked with tears.

"Oh, for the love of magic," Lucian complained. "These rituals will be my undoing."

Leonidas laughed, but it seemed a little choked. Then he reached out and grasped hold of Lucian's shoulder. "My brother, just wait until you go before our mother."

"Waiting sounds like an excellent plan. Perhaps until after the birth."

Leonidas truly laughed then. And when he hugged Arabella this time, there was not a shred of jealousy in Lucian's body. Nothing but love and heartache.

His brother exited quickly, leaving Lucian alone with his treasure once more.

"My heart hurts for him," Arabella said after he was gone, her tears still flowing.

"One of the many reasons I love you." He was struck dumb with the realization that he had never actually uttered those words before.

He gathered her gently in his arms and held her for a long time after that.

Chapter Four

ARABELLA HAD BEEN PREGNANT FOR THREE WEEKS.

It was both the longest and shortest three weeks of her life—it stretched with endless rounds of mind-hazing sex, and yet, suddenly, she was halfway through what might be the last six weeks of her life.

If she even made it to the end. But right now, the most threatening part of her life was how she would make it through the next hour without her dress falling off in the most epically awful wardrobe failure of all time.

"I still think you should put your hair up," Rachel said as she wound a curler into Arabella's hair. She had invited Rachel to Lucian's lair to help get ready for the big presentation in front of the king and the queen and the entire House of Smoke.

Her and a barely-there dress that was held on mostly by magic.

Lucian had conjured it for her, and it seemed like a cross between French haute couture and medieval royalty. It was snug in the front, shoving up her breasts and making her look twice as endowed as she actually was—and the pregnancy had already pumped her up in that department. She appeared ridiculously voluptuous up top, then it was snug right down to her baby bump, then it flowed long, white billowing layers to the floor. A million of them, light as feathers floating in the breeze yet woven with crystals that sparkled in the afternoon sun. The sleeves were skinny and long, draping across the tops of her hands and then sporting long wing-like things that dropped to the floor. And the back... the back was basically non-existent. She was bare all the way down to her butt. If she moved the wrong way, she was certain she'd be mooning everyone in the royal court. Lucian said it was to show her seal—his mark on her, the writhing magical dragon tattooed on her back. It showed she was mated and carrying the baby prince. She got that, but she was both encased in fabric and bursting out of it.

And constantly afraid of falling out.

"This dress is insane," Arabella complained as Rachel tugged another roller into place. "I mean, it's beautiful, but damn, could my breasts be any more huge? I need my hair down to cover them up." In truth, even with her hair loose, it wouldn't provide anywhere near enough coverage.

"At least now we know which part of you Lucian likes best," Rachel said with a smirk.

"Oh, trust me, that's not his favorite part," Arabella deadpanned.

Rachel snorted and then laughed outright. "You guys still going at it like rabbits? I mean, Jesus, you've already made a baby. You can stop practicing now."

Arabella grinned. "I'm pretty sure Lucian will be banging me right up until the moment the baby is born. Something about it being good for the baby's health."

"Sure, sure." Rachel looked thoroughly unconvinced. "At least one of us is getting some action."

Arabella scowled, but before she could say anything, Cinaed poked his head into the bedroom. Technically, it was the guest room, but it was doubling as her prep room for the ceremony. Lucian didn't want her leaving the lair any more than necessary.

"Is there anything you need, my lady?" Cinaed asked.

"For the fourth time, Cinaed, I'm fine. Beat it."

His head disappeared from the crack in the doorway, and the door shut behind him.

"That guy can seriously be a pain in the ass," Rachel snarled.

"I'm sure it's not him," Arabella said, wincing as Rachel tugged another hot roller up tight against her scalp. "It's Lucian—he's sending Cinaed in to check on me every five minutes because he knows I'll just yell at him if he dares poke his head in here. But you know he hates for me to be alone."

"What the hell am I? Furniture?" Rachel tucked the last of the curlers in and crossed her arms.

Arabella reached up to squeeze her best friend's hand. "You are awesome. It's just that you're not a super strong dragon shifter with foot-long razor-sharp talons."

"Yes, because that would be useful for curling hair."

Arabella examined her friend in the mirror as they waited for the curlers to cool. "I keep thinking about Leonidas and Leksander, Lucian's brothers. How they're basically doomed and can't mate."

Rachel frowned and uncrossed her arms. "I

suppose that's kind of sad. But people can live without having a lifelong lover."

Arabella was pretty sure Rachel was talking about herself as much as the two dragon shifters. "Maybe. But it's different for dragons. If they mate, it extends their lives. That's at least half of why I'm carrying Lucian's child." She caressed the baby in her belly who responded with a little wiggle, which in turn sparked a tiny sizzle of magic deep inside her. It was like a little party going on inside her belly all the time with the baby growing so fast.

"You decided to do this death-defying baby thing just to save Lucian's life?" Rachel asked skeptically. "What about the treaty?"

"Well, there's that, too. But honestly... it's mostly because I'm just so damn in love with the guy." She turned to face Rachel, and the curlers pulled a little painfully at her hair. "If you love a man, and by mating with him you can extend his life—save his life—wouldn't you do it? Isn't that what love is?"

Rachel snorted. "As if I know what love is."

But Arabella wasn't going to let her get away with that. She put her hand on top of Rachel's, which was tucked up tight and hidden in her folded arms again. "That's bullshit, and you know it. You love me." She scowled at her best friend. "Don't say you don't."

"That's different."

"No, it's really not." Arabella scanned her friend's eyes because this was so important, not just for Cinaed, but for her friend too. "If you mate with a dragon, you extend his life. Think about it, Rachel… if you care for Cinaed… if he's the kind of man you could love…"

Rachel unlocked her arms and leaned back. "Oh no. You're not talking me into that man's bed! I've got my hands full just trying to take care of you and that baby of yours." She gestured to Arabella's belly. The baby seemed to sense the unease and gave a little lurch. An almost painful lurch.

Arabella's hand automatically went to her tummy. She rubbed it right where a little baby dragon foot was poking her. "Leonidas and Leksander can't have mates," Arabella said. "Leonidas has a curse and Leksander is in love with an angeling and, I don't know, apparently that's not a thing that happens between angels and dragons. Cinaed's just an ordinary dragon with none of those issues. And he's a good man, Rachel. He could be good for you. If you give him a chance."

"No way. End of discussion. We're done talking

about this." She took Arabella's shoulders and twisted her back around to face the mirror, then she started to pull out the curlers. None too gently, either. Arabella knew she was just trying to avoid the fact that Cinaed was always around, always taking care of Arabella... and Rachel, too. That he was nothing like all the men who had been assholes in her life before. Her best friend was having to work overtime to pretend like she didn't have feelings for the good, decent man who was caring for both of them. It was starting to annoy her. No, more than annoy her, it was starting to make her *angry*. Rachel knew how good things were with her and Lucian. Why did she have to be so stubborn and pretend it couldn't be that way for her and Cinaed?

Then Arabella wouldn't have to watch her best friend grow old and die while Arabella lived on and on. They were supposed to be best friends *for life*... why wouldn't Rachel even consider it?

Arabella's anger was really starting to get under her skin. Her face heated up.

"Ouch," she said as Rachel pulled a little too hard on the last curler, yanking it free. "You don't have to be so rough!" Her face suffused with even more heat. Arabella ran a hand across her forehead to wipe away the sweat. She lurched up out of her seat so she could turn around and give Rachel shit for hurting her... but then she was suddenly dizzy and had to grip the chair just to keep from tumbling to the floor.

Alarm lit up Rachel's face. "Are you okay?" Her hands were on Arabella's arm, holding her up.

"You just... you shouldn't pull... so hard." It was becoming hard for her to breathe, and she was hot—*so hot*. She gasped in air, and it felt like fire backdrafting through her lungs.

Rachel stared at her arm where she had an iron grip on her. "Oh my God, Arabella, you're on fire!"

"Fire?" Arabella looked dazedly at her dress, trying to find the flames Rachel was talking about. That must be why she was so hot. But how could there be flames on a magical dress? It was pretty but just too hot. *Too hot.* Arabella clawed at the dress, ripping the arms off and pulling the corset down. Her breasts flopped out just like she knew they would. *Fuck.* But it was just too hot... she wrestled with it, trying to get it off.

Rachel swore colorfully and left her alone, running off somewhere to do something that wasn't being helpful. Arabella staggered into the chair, gripping both arms to sit down and continue to battle the dress. If only she were a dragon and could magic these things away. She kept wrestling with it, half naked, and suddenly Cinaed appeared next to the chair.

"Oh my God!" Arabella flailed to cover her naked breasts. "What you... what you... doing?" For some reason, her mouth wouldn't work right.

"Oh no," Cinaed breathed. "Stand back!" he shouted to someone, but Arabella didn't know who. *Her?* No, she didn't think so.

Cinaed scooped her up in his arms. "Come with me!" he shouted. Arabella couldn't understand— why was he yelling at her?

"Where are you taking her!" That was Rachel. Somehow her best friend's voice seemed both distant and panicked.

Cinaed didn't answer, he just whisked her away to the bathroom attached to the guest bedroom. He set her on her feet, but Arabella could barely stand. Rachel appeared and held her up while Cinaed waved his hands at the bath. It was suddenly filled with lumpy water. How could water be lumpy? The question ricocheted around in her brain with no answer. Cinaed reached for her filmy dress and basically slashed it off her body.

She shrieked in shock and embarrassment.

Cinaed picked her up again and gently laid her in the bath.

Holy fuck, it was cold!

The cold shocked her system, running through and chasing after the fire that had been raging through her body. Her toes and fingers went numb almost instantly, then the icy coolness slowly seeped deeper and deeper into her system. Her teeth chattered, but her mind cleared. She felt the baby thrashing inside her, burning up in the same heat that was consuming her.

"No, no, no," she said as she rocked in the water, sloshing it and waving it across her belly so that the coolness would reach her baby inside. She could barely breathe, much less speak, and all of her focus was on getting the baby cool. It took a long, agonizing minute, but it happened. The baby started to settle, not thrashing the way he was before. She was stark naked in the ice bath, Cinaed kneeling at her side and Rachel standing over her with clenched fists and a look of terror on her face.

"I'm okay," Arabella chattered out between clenched teeth, mostly for Rachel's benefit. "I'm okay, okay."

"The fuck you are!" Rachel knelt down to feel Arabella's hands and then her arms and finally pressing the backs of her fingers against Arabella's cheeks. She was cold enough that even Rachel's fingers felt warm.

"S-s-see?" Arabella said. "The baby's okay too. I can feel it."

"*Jesus fucking Christ.*" Rachel turned an accusatory eye to Cinaed. "What the hell was that?"

He just shook his head. "I don't know." He stood, frowning. "If my lady is all right for the moment, I'll summon the prince—"

"*No!*" Arabella thrust a hand out to stop him, even though she couldn't reach him. "Don't tell Lucian. He'll only worry."

Cinaed face twisted up as if she'd suggested lopping off his own arm. "My lady," he gasped in pain. "Do not ask me to lie about this."

"If you love your prince, do *not* tell him that his lady love almost just died." Her voice shook, and she couldn't tell if it was more from anger or the cold. Or perhaps fear. "It was just a hot flash. Just a... a passing thing. It's gone now." She didn't know what she was saying. She didn't know anything about dragonlings or pregnancies or what could really go wrong. But she knew for certain that if she told Lucian about it, he would never let her out of his sight again, even though there was nothing he could do about it, no more than Cinaed could. And the worry would weigh him down with darkness. She didn't want anything to make him think she was Cara—*she wasn't.* She was going to survive this.

Cinaed's level of distress was epic.

Arabella couldn't do anything about that while she was naked in an ice bath. And she had to stay there until she was sure the last of the heat had died away, and her baby was okay.

"Rachel." Arabella's teeth chattered again. "Tell him."

Rachel recovered from her frozen look of horror and panic and jumped to her feet, whirling on Cinaed. "Don't you breathe a word!" She jabbed a finger at him. "You swore your allegiance to her, too!"

Cinaed's face crumpled at that. He returned his gaze to stare helplessly at Arabella.

"And quit staring at her!" Rachel was venting all her fears on Cinaed, Arabella could tell. But she couldn't worry about that right now. Her best friend scooped up the tattered remains of her dress and shoved it at Cinaed. "Make yourself useful and magic up another dress for her."

He reluctantly tore his worried gaze from Arabella and trained an angry look on Rachel.

"You *will* call me if she begins to heat again. *Immediately.*" The force of his gaze was enough to shock even Rachel out of her anger.

She nodded but didn't say anything.

With a last look for Arabella, he stalked from the bathroom, taking the dress with him.

A full-body shudder gripped Arabella and seemed to travel straight through to the baby in her belly. He twitched as well, but the fire was completely gone now.

Arabella grabbed the side of the tub and tried to find her feet—they were so numb, she could barely feel them. "Help me up," she said to Rachel.

Her friend's hands were toasty warm on her chilled skin.

"Holy fuck," Rachel hissed as she helped Arabella up. "You scared the shit out of me with that."

"Me too." With Rachel's help, Arabella managed to climb out of the bath. Just the warm air of the bathroom felt like a relief. "But I'm okay. Promise."

Rachel didn't look convinced.

"You'll have to fix my hair again, though. The king and queen are waiting for me."

Rachel just pursed her lips and hurried over to the towel rack to get one for her.

Arabella pulled in a deep breath and let it out slow. She was fine. The baby was fine. If it happened again, she knew to get to an ice bath super fast. Not stand around wondering what the hell was happening.

But it spooked her something awful, and she could see the shadow of fear in Rachel's tight expression, too. But there was nothing to do about it now.

She just had to keep marching forward.

Three more weeks…

Chapter Five

ARABELLA WAS OVERDUE TO THE THRONE ROOM, AND it was making Lucian's runes twitch.

He had reached out with his fae senses not ten minutes ago, but she was fine. Still in the guest room of his lair, probably nervous about making her debut in front of the entire House. There was no cause for alarm, but he couldn't help his worry.

"She's fine, my brother," Leonidas said, standing next to Lucian and adjusting the cuffs on his jacket. "I've sensed her in the hallways. She'll be here momentarily."

Leksander eyed Lucian but said nothing.

He just gave them both a gruff nod, wearing his impatience like a shield to keep their questions at bay.

The throne room was resplendent with all the ethereal décor that magic could provide from flickering torch lights to bouquets of flowers in every nook to velvet-draped walls and floors. The long, narrow room was seldom used, and in fact, Lucian couldn't recall a time it had been put to use in the hundred years since they had relocated to the Seattle mountains.

Just after Cara's death.

The last time the House of Smoke had seen such a ceremony, it was back in France, and Lucian was waiting for Cara to make her appearance in her presentation dress, the one he had specially conjured to her precise specifications. After her death, he could no longer bear to live in his own lair. To walk the same halls that she had. To live inside the same keep where she died. It had driven him away from France and eventually brought the entire House here. This new throne room in Seattle was constructed to be identical to the one they left behind, still steeped in the history of their House, but it was left fallow, literally waiting until someone extraordinary could take Cara's place.

He banished that from his mind.

There would be no thoughts of the dead today.

Lucian and his brothers stood by the door,

awaiting Arabella's arrival. *His mate. The mother of his child.* She should be the only focus today. Her coming out to the House was the most solemn of occasions, and the one his mother had been insisting he make as soon as Arabella passed her fortnight of seclusion.

His mother and father sat on their thrones at the far end of the room opposite the door. King Larik and Queen Alexis, both dragons nearing the end of their lives at a thousand years. The dragons of the House lined either side, standing and waiting for Arabella's arrival. Everyone was dressed in traditional formalwear, a mixture of ancient dragon culture and the medieval period in which his mother and father had been born as well as Lucian and his brothers. Most in attendance were male dragons, but the few mated ones had brought their females to the ceremony. The queen was beautifully regal in her purple gown, fitted and flowing, elegance and beauty, as always. The king wore the traditional high collar and long black jacket, etched with fine gold thread. Lucian's presentation attire was more elaborate, suitable for his station as the crown prince for the ceremony. His black hood was pushed back, and the drape of his long tunic was woven with protective wedding runes, the same that he had conjured in Arabella's gown. His chest was emblazoned with the dragon of their House.

His sensitive hearing caught the whisper of Arabella's steps outside the door of the throne room just before Cinaed swung open the door. His best friend was somber as he held the door wide for Lucian's mate. He only had a moment to wonder about the furrowed look on Cinaed's face before Lucian's mind was captured by the sight of Arabella in her presentation dress. Halfway through her pregnancy now, the bump of her belly sweetly round and captivating, she radiated every fertility symbol worshiped through all of time. Flowing layers of white fabric floated around her as she moved. Her sweet breasts perched high, her delicately freckled skin making his mouth ache. A single golden band wrapped around her temple, signaling her new status as a princess. The flowing train of white floated in the breeze behind her. He was so captivated by her appearance that it took a moment for his eyes to find hers. But when they did, those green jewels locked onto him, and she bestowed upon him a tentative smile.

If only he could capture her in this moment and

never let go. If only it didn't require her to risk her life to bring her to his throne room. If only the specter of Cara's death didn't loom over her, the sparkle in Arabella's eyes just the same as Cara's when she had come through the door all those years ago. Lucian ground his teeth and forced himself to push those thoughts aside. There was no room for them here today, in this moment.

Cinaed held the door as Arabella stepped through. Her maid, Rachel, followed. Leonidas left Lucian's side to offer his arm to Arabella. Tradition held that a dragon sponsor would escort his mate before the king and queen to present her for their official blessing. It was a formality for matings which had already occurred, but Leonidas had insisted that he fulfill the role. Not that Arabella had any objection whatsoever. The two of them marched in a solemn, measured pace down the length of the throne room. Rachel followed a step behind, fussing with the long train that flowed behind Arabella, even though the magic imbued in the dress kept it floating perfectly. Smiles and glittering eyes of appreciation followed Arabella. Her sealing mark undulated along her back, drawing everyone's murmurs of approval. It was seductive, all that skin, all marked by him, her beauty and strength all perfectly shown off by that alluring showcase. Lucian could feel the twin emotions of pride and jealous lust rippling through the entire assemblage of male dragons.

Their prince was mated once again—something many of them surely never expected to happen— and to a beauty who was plainly extraordinary. They had much to envy, but even their piercing gazes didn't arouse any jealousy in Lucian. There were a hundred or so of them, and not one would wish for anything but the safe delivery of his drag- onling into the world, securing the treaty along with the House of Smoke's place in the immortal world for another generation.

Cinaed joined Lucian and Leksander by the door once he had closed it. They would wait until Arabella's acceptance before making their own solemn march down the length of the throne room for the final blessing by the king and queen.

A glance at Cinaed showed his worried look was still present. His gaze was locked on Arabella, who had nearly reached the throne dais. Or perhaps it was Rachel's lovely rear end that captured his atten- tion as she skittered and shuffled along behind, bending to adjust the dress that didn't need adjust- ment. Even as Lucian had been buried in his own concerns, it had not escaped his notice that Cinaed gladly hewed close to Rachel. And Lucian recognized lust in another dragon when he saw it.

"You should grab hold of love when it comes your way, my friend," Lucian whispered, dipping his head to Cinaed. Arabella's introduction up front was continuing apace without them.

Cinaed gave him an odd look—and a more tentative one than Lucian expected. Was he truly that hesitant to bed the female? Or was there more to it than that?

Cinaed looked back to the front, this time plainly fixed on Rachel standing off to the side while Arabella held court with the king and queen. "I'm holding out for the rare human woman capable of loving a dragon such as myself." Then he turned back to Lucian. "Knowing the price she might pay for that love."

Lucian's heart squeezed. Cinaed had been at his side through everything with Cara, from the first blush of love through to the tragic and bloody end. And that dark time when Lucian had banished himself to the dim forests of Europe, seeking a redemption that would not come. It was only through the forbearance and steady love of his friend that Lucian had found his way out of the wildness once again.

"Any woman who wins your heart," Lucian said, "is a treasure indeed. And you're still a young dragon. What have you, a hundred years under your scales? Mating now would cut your life short, and I want to see you live a long and full life, my friend."

Cinaed grimaced. "I care not for that. I care for finding the *right* woman. The one who wins my heart would have it forever, or as many years as the fates grant me." Cinaed's gaze drew forward again, but this time, it landed on Leonidas. "The House of Smoke has blessed me. I've learned the lessons of your brother well. He was unwilling to mate as a young dragon, and he paid the price for it. With all due respect, my prince, I am not that foolish."

Lucian smiled. "You are the wisest dragon I know, Cinaed. Woe to the woman who crosses you."

Cinaed just shook his head and stared at the floor. "Woe to me with my foolish tendency to fall in love all too quickly."

"Love, you say?" Lucian examined Rachel once again, standing at attention by Arabella's side. Even from this distance, Lucian could see the tears trickling from the corners of her eyes, clearly with love for her friend.

"It makes no sense," Cinaed said with a grimace. "She's quarrelsome and angry and far too quick to tell me where I'm wrong."

Lucian barely stifled his laugh. "Sounds perfect for you."

Cinaed drew back. "Surely my lord jests."

"Not at all." Lucian smirked. "It's the ones you cannot possibly stay away from, the ones who irritate you the most... those are the ones who find their way deep into your heart and never let go."

Cinaed briefly squeezed his eyes shut and shook his head. "That's what I fear."

Lucian rested a hand on Cinaed's shoulder. "Don't fear love, my friend. Learn that lesson from me."

Cinaed bit his lip and seemed to be conceding the point, but then he said, "I fear giving my heart to the wrong woman. I'm willing to wait for the right one. I've no need to jump at the first one that makes my blood boil and my irritation swell and who inspires me to more than simply drag her off to my bed."

Lucian smiled. "Anyone who loves my Arabella cannot be all bad."

With that, Cinaed's face opened in recognition. "My lord may be on to something there."

"Indeed." He clapped his hand again on Cinaed's shoulder, but the time had come for him to approach the throne. Silence reigned throughout the room, heavy with expectation.

Lucian led the way with Cinaed and Leksander trailing behind him. Arabella had stepped to the side with a radiant expression awaiting him. He fought to shove away the sensation of déjà vu, that he had been in this moment before with Cara. Instead, he focused on Arabella's beaming face, letting her draw him in as she always did. Only when he reached the front did he turn his gaze to his mother, who was likewise beaming, and his father's wide smile.

"Your majesties," he said with a low bow. "What is your decision?" It was a formality, but formalities and ritual had power. Their approval would cement Arabella's place in the House of Smoke and in the eyes of every dragon present.

"Your mate's love is True," his mother said, speaking first, as was custom. "I accept her into our House."

Then his father spoke next, his deep booming voice only slightly touched with gravel and age.

"Her strength and good heart are a blessing upon this House." His father's words had a double-edged meaning for Lucian now. The same words had been spoken when Cara was accepted, but they proved not to be true. She was *not* strong enough to survive him and his seed. Her heart was good... but not good enough. Not with the doubts that must have lingered there. "I accept her into the House of Smoke," his father continued. Then he raised his voice. "May your dragonling live long, and may the House of Smoke prosper under the blessing of a new prince."

That was the signal, along with the king's raised hands.

The House was holding their breath, waiting.

Arabella didn't know it, but the ceremony was sealed with a kiss. Lucian held his hand out to her, and when she took it, he pulled her close. With one hand on her belly and his son and the other in her hair, he brought her in for a kiss that was delicious and divine and sparked everywhere through him.

And it was a damn good thing they were heading back to his lair immediately afterward.

A roar of approval went up throughout the throne room, and Lucian let his kiss linger and linger, only releasing her when he sensed a flush of embarrassment running through her cheeks.

He grinned as he pulled away. "Welcome to the House of Smoke, Princess Arabella."

The blush that was tinging her cheeks red and making her eyes flutter was almost as captivating as her kiss.

"Lucian," she said, her voice a little breathy. "Take me home."

He frowned, a spike of fear lancing through his heart and bursting the glory of the moment. "Are you all right?"

She took his hand again and squeezed it. "Yes. Just…" Her gaze roamed the still-cheering House of dragons. They were putting their enthusiasm into applause and backslapping and rounds of chanting Arabella's name. "Just a little overwhelmed."

His fear subsided. He turned quickly to his parents. "By your leave, your majesties, my mate cannot wait to retire to my lair."

His father grinned, and even his mother had a knowing smile.

When Lucian turned back to Arabella, she looked stricken. "Oh my God, Lucian," she whispered hoarsely. He smirked and swept her into his arms and carried her out through the cheering crowd, toward the back of the throne room and, eventually, his lair.

With all the ceremonies behind them, he had every intention of making love to Arabella for the remaining three weeks of her pregnancy pretty much continuously.

Woe to any dragon who interrupted them.

Chapter Six

"Okay, these little, tiny, baby clothes are just fucking cute." Rachel's running commentary made Arabella laugh out loud.

"This why I need you here, helping me sort this stuff out. Lucian can't even look at the clothes."

Rachel scrunched up her face. "Oh. Yeah. Because of the baby before."

Arabella nodded. It squeezed her heart every time she thought about it—she could hardly even imagine what it was doing to Lucian. She held up a tiny jumper suit that was red with little hooks and buttons to hold the shoulder straps down. "How cute is this?"

Rachel scrutinized the tiny clothing. "Maximum cuteness. Illegally cute."

"Perfect." Arabella set it in the pile of keepers. She sighed before going on to the next one. "The only solution is for me to just have the baby, Rach. *To live.* That's the only thing that will prove all of Lucian's fears wrong."

"Well, you'll get no argument from me on that." She held up another tiny suit set, this one a miniature replica of Lucian's formal attire, complete with a tiny emblazoned gold-thread dragon. "Although no baby is going to be happy wearing this getup."

Arabella giggled, and the baby kicked with the motion. Her hand reflexively went to her belly and soothed that spot by rubbing it. "As if you know anything about babies."

Rachel scowled. "Hey, I've been reading up. I'm going to be a fucking expert on this by the time the baby gets here. Not that you're giving me much time, mind you."

It was true. She was already almost four weeks into the six-week pregnancy… and she was starting to get big. That hadn't slowed down her love-making with Lucian, but they had to get a little more creative. He was out in the great room now with Cinaed and Leonidas, awaiting the fashion show, once Arabella and Rachel had made their selections from the vast quantity of clothing

Cinaed had conjured for them. Arabella had barely managed to banish Lucian from the room—he still was clinging to her side every moment. Most of the time, that was delicious and sexy, but occasionally she needed some room to breathe. And time to go through baby clothes he couldn't stand to look at. And a visit with her best friend in her apartment—technically still the guest apartment, but Rachel had started decorating it with Cinaed's help.

This was just the kind of break she needed.

"So, how are things going with Cinaed?" Arabella asked with feigned casualness.

"Oh, don't even get started with me on that." Rachel scowled and rifled through a pile of clothes they had yet to even touch. "I specifically asked him to conjure some non-primary-color suits, and there's nothing here that's even close to pastel yellow."

Arabella shook her head and chuckled.

"What?" asked Rachel, indignant. "You'd think the man could honor a simple request."

"Do you guys fight over *everything?*" Arabella asked with a smirk. "Still?"

"That man has too many opinions," Rachel grumbled.

Arabella laughed outright at that. "Right. Sure."

Rachel stuck her tongue out at her, then pulled a tiny train conductor suit from the pile. "Why do you want me to hook up with that guy, anyway? I'm keeping my eyes on the prize here, Ari. Which is *you*. And the baby." She held up the train suit. "I'm thinking this thing has gotta go in the *no* pile."

"Agreed." Arabella sighed and then twitched a little as the baby kicked.

Rachel's sharp-eyed gaze noticed right away. "You okay?"

Arabella waved it off. "Yeah, fine. The baby gets more active every day. He just likes jumping around in there."

Rachel scowled. "I'm sorry, but that's gotta be a little strange, right? I mean…" She waved her hand in the general direction of Arabella. "It's like you've got some kind of alien moving around inside you. It's every horror movie you've ever seen."

Arabella smirked. "Someday, when you have your own dragonling, you'll understand."

Her best friend gave her a look like she was crazy. "Not going to happen."

A flush of heat washed through Arabella. She sucked in a breath and blew it out slowly. The waves had been hitting a little more frequently lately. For no reason at all, that she could tell. It wasn't like they came when she was more active, or stressed out, or whatever. She could be just sitting on the bed like she was now, and one would just subtly ramp up, heating her body in a wave, and then recede. She didn't even mention them, not anymore, to Rachel. Or anyone else, really. Especially not Lucian. They would just get worried looks on their faces, and there wasn't anything to be done about them unless they were super serious like that one time. Then she would say something. But she didn't want them to get worked up unnecessarily. Or have Cinaed rip off her clothes and send her into an ice bath unless, and until, that was required.

Rachel didn't even notice with the way she was flinging little outfits right and left off the pile on the bed. She got to the bottom and declared, "Okay, I'm going to fucking kill the man. No pastels. Zero. Zip. Nada." She straightened up and planted her hands on her hips, staring hard at the offending pile.

Oh dear. "Aren't *I* the one who's supposed to get irrationally upset about crazy stupid things?" Arabella asked. "You know, pregnancy hormones, and all that?" The truth was, she couldn't care less about the little clothes. They were just an excuse to spend some time with Rachel.

But her best friend was taking it to a Defcon One level of seriousness.

She stomped over to the door, pulled it open, and shouted out into the great room, "Cinaed, you double crossing dragon, get in here!"

Arabella laughed so hard, she had to hold her side to keep it from jiggling too much.

A moment later, Cinaed appeared at the door, looking incensed. "By all that's magic, woman, what is the fuss you're raising now?" He threw a sharp glance at Arabella, but the giggles that were hiccupping out of her made his shoulders relax.

"There are no pastels," Rachel said like this was a crime against humanity.

Cinaed turned an angry glare back to her. "And this is a thing worthy of embarrassing me in front of my prince?"

"Well, if you did your damn job—"

"Oh, for the love of God..." Arabella could barely speak she was laughing so hard. "Cinaed, just come in and make some more clothes. Please."

Cinaed gritted his teeth but stepped into the room and closed the door. "What color does my lady desire?" he asked Rachel pointedly.

"Pastels. Babies are supposed to wear nice pastel-type colors. Anyone knows that."

Arabella was starting to gasp with laughter and had to fan herself with one of the tiny t-shirts. She hadn't laughed so hard in some time, and the idea that Rachel had any clue what babies were actually supposed to wear was giving her the terminal giggles.

"Very well." Cinaed went to work and conjured a tiny yellow jumper. More sunflower than Easter egg, though. "Like this?"

"No!" Rachel scowled at him. "Are you color-blind?" She turned to Arabella. "Is that a dragon thing? Can he legitimately just not see the colors at all?"

"Oh God," Arabella gasped, trying to stop the laughter but being completely unsuccessful.

"I can see color just fine," Cinaed ground out. "How about this?" He conjured five more identical outfits in varying shades of yellow. "Surely my lady can find one to her suiting amongst these."

Arabella fanned herself harder and tried to rein herself in. Then another one of those waves of heat came over her. Her laughter was choked off as the wave didn't simply rise and fall but seemed to catch wind and wash over and sweep her under.

"Rachel," she gasped out, struggling for breath between the leftover spasms of laughter and the new wave of burning fire that seemed to be flooding her body.

"No, no!" Rachel said, wagging a finger at her without looking at her. "Let the dragon explain himself why precisely *none* of these are actually pastel."

"Rach..." The gasp in her voice finally drew both of their attentions.

"Oh my God!" Rachel threw out her hands in surprise, then launched herself across the room and, in two fast strides, reached Arabella's side.

"My lady!" Cinaed was a half step behind her.

"It's the heat," Arabella panted. "Need... ice bath... quick!"

He snatched her up from the bed and carried her into the bathroom, holding her with one hand and conjuring as he went with the other. By the time they reached the bath, it was already filled with ice water, and he plunged her into it. It was like an icy storm crashing into her body, but the heat was so extreme it wasn't reaching her. She stared at the water as it started to hiss around her body, boiling up steam that tossed around the ice cubes.

Cinaed just stared, aghast. "Holy mother of magic." His voice was just a whisper.

Rachel stood in the doorway with both hands over her mouth and panic in her eyes.

"Get the prince!" Cinaed shouted, panic filling his voice as well.

Rachel jumped and turned to flee, but Arabella could see her through the doorway, and she didn't get halfway through the room before the door burst open, crashing into the wall and coming half off its hinges. Lucian barreled through, shoved her aside, and launched himself into the bathroom.

"Arabella." His voice was a gasp. He fell to his knees beside the bath.

"Too hot," she cried out. And that was all she could say because the fire had reached her lungs and was closing them down. Her whole body was an inferno, and her baby was thrashing with it. She could see his tiny feet and hands poking against her stomach from the inside. Making her skin undulate and stretch, as if he was trying to claw his way out. To escape the heat. The first race of fear reached her heart as it pumped madly to counteract the heat surge.

Was this it? Was this how she died?

"No, no, no." Lucian's hands were on her,

finding the bare skin at the back of her neck and placing another in the ice water, palm flat on her belly. "I have you, my love. I have you." But the panic in his voice was not reassuring. The runes were skittering down his arms to his hands, and Arabella could feel it, like icy fingers were reaching into her, penetrating the blazing hot surface of her skin.

Leonidas appeared at the side of the bath. "Let me help, my brother," he said in a steely voice rasped with urgency. He reached his hands to her— one to hold her cheek, the other to join his brother's at her belly. His runes danced along his skin as well. The icy fingers reach deeper inside her, doing battle against the magical heat that was burning throughout her.

"What happened?" Lucian threw the angry words over his shoulder at Cinaed.

Cinaed held up his hands, helpless. "Nothing, my lord, I swear. She was just suddenly overcome. It was much faster this time—" He cut himself off, his eyes wide.

"This time." The rage in Lucian's voice made the cool slivers battling the heat in her belly dim a little.

"Focus, brother," Leonidas ground out. "There will be time for recriminations later."

Lucian swung his attention back to her, and she could see the fear in his eyes. "I'm not losing you," he vowed, and she felt the renewed strength in the magic he was pumping into her.

She reached up to his cheek with her hand, which was shaking. When she touched him, it was like his skin was a thousand degrees cooler than hers. "Not today," she managed, but she wasn't entirely sure.

Behind Lucian, Rachel was screeching something at Cinaed. The heat had reached into Arabella's mind and was making it difficult for her to piece the words together. Then Rachel started beating her hands on Cinaed's chest and cursing at him.

The words finally came through. "You fucking dragons! Fucking men! You always get what you want, even if women have to die for it!"

I'm not going to die. But Arabella couldn't make her mouth form the words.

Cinaed pulled her to him, wrapping his arms around her and holding her. She was sobbing into his chest, and he was saying something to her. Something about not being afraid. Something about the magic of love.

The magic of love. Arabella brought her focus back to her baby in her womb, still kicking and thrashing under the fire that was threatening to consume him. She focused on the icy tendrils of magic that were trying to work their way deep inside her. She urged the magic on, coupling it with every ounce of love she had for her baby. *You have to live, my little one. You have to live. You have all my love, and all your father's love, and an entire House of love.* She felt her lips move, whispering the words without sound because she had no breath left to spare. But it was working. She could feel the icy magic sinking deeper and deeper, calming the baby, soothing her body.

But it had taken everything she had to give.

Her head lolled back. She would've slipped under the water if Lucian and Leonidas's hands weren't holding her up. She couldn't keep her eyes open any longer, every ounce of energy having gone into boosting the magic they were giving her to save her child.

"It's okay," she gasped. "It's going to be okay." She wasn't sure if it made any sound.

Then she drifted off into a sea of blackness.

Chapter Seven

IT WAS ANOTHER TEN MINUTES BEFORE LUCIAN WAS willing to take her out of the bath.

An hour before her temperature dropped down to normal. Normal for a dragon's mate, at least. And an agonizing two more hours while she thrashed in some kind of dream state, alternating moans and mumbling. He couldn't decide if they were from pain or pleasure. He brought her back to his lair, changed her into dry clothes, and made her as comfortable as he could. It didn't seem to matter.

He never left her side, feeling each small torment as a strike against his heart.

Finally, in the greatest gush of relief he'd ever known… Arabella opened her eyes.

At first, Lucian couldn't speak. He just stroked

her hair and gazed in wonder at her beautiful, green eyes. She blinked in confusion and sleepiness at him. She was curled up on his bed—*their* bed—the covers twisted underneath her.

"Water," she said, then coughed.

His heart seized. He'd never run so fast as he did to the bathroom and back, returning with a small paper cup that half sloshed on the bed before he managed to get it to her. She was struggling to sit up, so he helped her, once the cup was secure in her hands. They were shaking, but just a little.

It could have been worse. So much worse.

He held her while she gulped it down.

"More." She handed it back to him, but at least now her voice sounded more normal.

He ran again, returning with two cups. She drank them both and slowly seemed to come back to him. He couldn't help pulling her into his lap again, stroking her hair while she drank and just *touching* her—gently, softly, sparking magic and, he hoped, pleasure—anything to revive her and reassure himself that she was truly okay.

Then he girded himself for the words that had to come next. Because he was dead certain that doubts about him had brought this on, and he was determined to head this off, air whatever the issues were… before they could literally kill her.

Just as he mustered the courage to speak, she cut him off by crumpling the cups, tossing them over the side of the bed, and taking his face in both hands… and kissing him.

It was so surprising—and welcome—that he was instantly lost in it.

His hands wove into her hair, and his mouth reveled in hers. How he wished this was all that was required—that she could just know of his love by his touch. But obviously that wasn't enough. And kissing her, in spite of her fervent exploration of his chest with her hands, was an indulgence he couldn't afford.

He pulled back from the kiss.

"Arabella." His voice choked, and he stroked her hair again as he searched for words. "You have to tell me what caused this."

She frowned. "Nothing caused it."

"Is it the other women?" he asked, his chest tight.

She pulled back and gaped at him. "What other women?"

Oh, fuck. He gritted his teeth and forced it out. "The ones in Seattle. That night when I… when I thought I might force myself to… to mate with someone else. Cinaed told me you found out. That you thought—"

But she was rolling her eyes at him. *"Lucian."* She pursed her lips.

He held his breath.

"Did you sleep with them?" she asked.

"No," he said quickly. Maybe too quickly.

She raised one eyebrow.

"I swear upon my honor, Arabella, I did not…" He swallowed. "I did not technically have sex with them. It didn't get that far. But I did… there was a brief time of…" *Sweet magic,* why couldn't he force the words out?

"You messed around." Her face was set like a stone.

"Yes." He would sooner have spilled blood—a great quantity of blood—than utter that word.

"Did you enjoy it?"

"No!"

The arched eyebrow again. "Not even a little?"

"No. I just… I was trying to seduce them and…"

Both her eyebrows went up.

He hurried his words. "I was trying to seduce them and cause them pleasure, but there was none there for me. None except…" He swallowed again, ready to drown on these words. "Only when I was picturing *you*, my love. When it was *you* I was touching, only then did I have a fleeting moment of…" His mouth was working, but no more words were coming out.

Her face twisted with emotion, which confused him… and then she snorted a kind of ungracious laugh and shook her head. Which perplexed him completely.

Had the fever demented her? Had it stolen her mind?

She smiled wide, and it made him want to hide under the bed. "For the love of magic, Arabella," he said, aghast. "Why are you laughing at me?"

That just made her laugh some more. She covered her mouth with her hand. "Sorry!" she mumbled behind it. "I'm sorry." The smile tamed a little, but the laugh still danced in her eyes. "It's just that I can completely see it. It's so totally *you*, Lucian."

"What on earth do you mean?" Horror was squeezing down on his chest. This felt so completely unmoored from reality, he had no idea what was happening.

She spread her hands wide, the smile returning.

"You were so determined to do what's right—what's noble and good and true—that you pushed away the woman you love so she wouldn't get hurt." She rested her hand on her belly, patting it in a loving way that captured his heart. "You couldn't bear to see the people you love—another woman, another child—suffer, so you gave up everything. The chance at another five hundred years of life. The chance to be *happy*, even if only for a short while. You even tried to kill yourself—death by vampire!—all to keep me safe. Why? Because *you love me*, Lucian Smoke. I've known it from that first night you pushed me away, and I know it now with more certainty than any woman on earth has ever known such a thing."

He just stared at her, amazed. How did this woman see so straight into his soul?

She dipped her head and gave him a mock scolding look. "You tried to run away from me, Lucian. You tried *so hard* to leave me to keep me safe. But even in the arms of other women, even in your dogged determination to fulfill your duty to the House of Smoke, you couldn't help but think of *me*. You couldn't help but love me. *Still.*"

It was true. All of it.

He reached a hand out to touch her cheek—her

skin sparked magic, and he was immeasurably relieved that it was the same temperature as his. "My love, there has to be something that caused the dragonfire to rage inside you. Some doubt you have about me, about our love—"

"I'm *not* having any doubts, Lucian!"

It pained him to press on, but he had to. *"Think,* my sweet Arabella. Is there some dark corner of your mind that worries about... something. Anything. Whatever it is, we have to find it and banish it. *Please, Arabella.* I can't lose you... or the baby..." Emotion was choking him as he begged.

She sat up straighter on the bed, propped against the mound of pillows at the head, and crossing her legs to cradle her beautifully rounded belly. *Their son.*

She was getting comfortable, but the look on her face was livid. "I am *not* losing this baby! You are *not* going to lose me. You need to knock this shit off, Lucian, because you're starting to piss me off."

"Arabella, I almost lost you *just now!"*

"That wasn't anything *I* did," she threw at him, defensively. "It just flares up for no reason."

"It's *not* for no reason, my love. There has to be a reason. Just tell me what it is. I don't want it to fester and then flare up and then steal you both from me just like…" He stopped himself cold.

"Just like Cara." Her eyes narrowed.

"I didn't mean…" He didn't know what he meant.

"I am *not* your dead mate, Lucian." Her face was pinking up, almost turning red with her anger, which struck a cold, dead fear through Lucian's heart.

"No, my love, you're not." His voice was a chastened whisper.

Her fists were balled up, and she looked ready to pummel him. And she was biting her lip hard, as if she had words to say, but was holding them back.

"Whatever you have to say, my treasure… *say it.*" He braced himself.

She chewed on her lip some more.

He waited.

Finally, she said, "Do you know why Cara died?"

He blinked. It was possibly the last thing he expected out of her mouth. "I… I killed her…" He couldn't breathe. Was this what she feared? That he would repeat that horror with her? *"Arabella.* I'd sooner fall on an angel blade than… I would never…"

But she waved him off. "Of course not. That's not what I'm saying. I'm saying *do you know?* What *really* killed her?"

For the second time, he wondered if the fever had taken her mind when it left. He just stared at her.

"It was Zephan." The biting cold of her voice speared right through him.

"*What?*" he sputtered. "Arabella, I was there. I lived through—"

"*No.*" She clambered up on her knees, her hands gripping his shoulders for support as she balanced on the bed, face to face, holding him prisoner with her intense gaze. "You tried to *save* her. But the thing that was killing her—the wound in her soul—that was caused by Zephan. I love you, Lucian Smoke, but I have something I have to tell you. You *have* to understand this."

He just nodded because he had no idea what she was talking about.

"Zephan seduced Cara."

"*What?*" He drew back, but her hands were locked hard on his shoulders, not letting him go. "That's not possible..." But the trickle of recognition was already worming its way into his mind. Cara had changed—before the fever, before the baby tried to fight its way out of her body—something had happened, and she had fallen into a terrible despair. All along, Lucian had believed that was the point at which she had begun to doubt his love for her, despite his fervent reassurances. He never knew *why*. He never knew what triggered it.

"I'm sorry," Arabella was saying, again and again. "I'm sorry to be the one to tell you. I don't know how exactly it happened, but Zephan raped her. That fucking mental rape thing he does where he makes you want it. It's fucking horrible, and it wasn't her fault. Believe me, I *know* that. But afterward, I'm sure it just flat-out destroyed her, from the inside out. That was his intent with it. He didn't want to fuck her. He may be a fae prince, but he's just like every other abusive rapist I've seen in my practice—he wanted to *hurt* her. *Control her.* And he did it in the most devastating way possible. I'm sure she felt like she couldn't tell you—that's just how rape victims are. It messes with your head. I've seen it so many times. And *that*… that's what triggered her doubts. That's what killed her, Lucian."

The horror of it truly seized him. "I failed to protect her." All the pain was coming surging back. All the dark horror of it. "I failed to keep the fae from her."

"No." She gripped his face in her hands, forcing him to look at her. "You failed to keep the fae from me as well. He's fucking *powerful,* Lucian. You couldn't have stopped him. And now, with me, he's been doing everything he can to drive us apart. But you know what? *He failed."*

Lucian blinked, still being pulled into that blackness he fell into after Cara died. "He failed?"

Arabella spoke through gritted teeth. "He tried to seduce me—fucking *twice* with his mental games and his glamour—and I was able to resist. Able to see through it, somehow. I don't know how... except I know that my love for you is *real.* This whole thing about True Love? I believe in that like you can't even imagine, because I've seen it work. *Felt it,* Lucian. Even now, even as the dragonfire was consuming me, do you know what stopped it?"

"What?" He was held captive by her words.

"Love." She said it fiercely, like a quiet battle cry. "My love for you and this baby of ours has a magic all its own—a *powerful* magic—and that love reached inside me and quenched that fire. You and Leonidas helped, but I had to make that final leap myself. And I could because my love for you is True, through and through. *That's why it worked.* Don't you see?"

He was nodding with her words—because of course, they made sense. True Love was a force unto itself, but when bound to the magic of the treaty, it carried a fae level of magical power. But he was struck mute by what she was saying. How could he have not seen this before?

"You are *mine*, Lucian Smoke. I've known it from the beginning. I don't love you for what you do, but for *who you are*. This broken, noble man—a person so good, he'd rather fall on an angel blade than cause me any pain. I didn't even know someone like you could exist. But now that I do, I've claimed you for my own, and I am *never* letting you go. Now knock off this business of doubting my love for you! That's never going to change, and you're stuck with me."

Tears threatened his eyes, and his hands had minds of their own, sliding fast up into her hair and pulling her face to him. He kissed her, again and again, and with such need, such love, that he felt he might die just from the completeness of it. It wrecked him, body and soul, and he dared to hope, for the very first time, that this might actually be his life. He might truly have won her.

That she might live after all.

"I don't deserve you," he whispered against her

cheek as he brushed his lips there, across her jaw, down her neck…

"Well, you have me anyway," she said with a light laugh in her voice that made his heart soar.

"Not the way I want," he said, a huskiness in his voice speaking his meaning for him.

"Oh?" she asked, tipping her head back to give him better access to her neck, where his gentle kisses were quickly turning more fervent as he tasted her and nipped at her delicious body. "How do you want me?"

"Naked at the edge of my bed," he said hoarsely. He magicked away her clothes and his, and then lifted her bottom, gentle with her rounded belly between them, but determined to tip her back and move her into a position where he could take her as quickly as possible. His need to be inside her had never been so urgent.

She grasped hold of his shoulders as he laid her back. Then she captured his gaze with those brilliant green eyes. "Don't hold back, Lucian Smoke."

He groaned his need for her, sliding her hips to the edge of the bed and kneeling to line his already rock-hard cock up with her entrance. His hands found her skin—one gentle on the mound of her belly, the other gripping her hip hard for when he would take her. But he knew that she wasn't just asking him to take her hard, the way she liked… she was asking him not to hold back his heart from her any longer.

And that was a thing that he—finally and with heart-lifting abandon—felt he could give.

Completely.

Chapter Eight

L<small>UCIAN WAS POISED TO THRUST THAT BIG, GORGEOUS</small> cock of his inside her...

...and hesitating.

She was about to let loose some very determined cursing about this not being the time nor place for his teasing, but the words he whispered stopped her complaints before they could get out.

"I'll never doubt your love again," he said. "And I'll never hold back. You own me completely, Arabella Sharp. I am yours."

Then, kneeling at the side of the bed, holding her legs up with his ridiculously strong arms, he thrust into her, filling her suddenly and completely. With the baby getting so big, she could hardly do much but lie back and enjoy it. Which she did—

thoroughly. This mated sex thing was impossibly erotic. Every stroke sparked magical pleasure along the length of him inside her. Every momentary contact—his hands gripping her hips, his cock sliding deep, his body banging on her sensitive nub —sparked electric pleasure-inducing magic. He'd just started and already the first orgasm was tightening, coiling deep inside her and building toward a blessed release. One she was desperate for after the harrowing events of the afternoon.

Surviving a near-death experience was impossibly making the sex even *better*— not that she ever wanted to repeat any of the first part.

Lucian was groaning and grunting and pounding her hard, just as she liked it. Now that her body was immortal, it was as if she craved the full measure of whatever he could dish out—harder thrusting, deeper angles, bites that stopped just short of leaving marks. Somehow the rougher sex was even more erotic knowing how gentle and loving Lucian truly was. It was all for her. All for her pleasure. And now that he truly wasn't holding back anymore, his fervent thrusts and groans were rocketing her toward release. Then his thumb found her nub and started flicking. She shrieked with the pleasure-sparked surge that set off, and then she came so hard, it lifted her bottom off the bed to meet his continuing thrusts. Her body convulsed with pleasure, and she just bucked with it, lost in what he was giving her—*himself.* Completely and totally.

This was what she had risked everything for.

This was what her life would be like forever— whether five minutes or five hundred years, this bliss of owning Lucian Smoke's heart completely was *hers.*

She was barely past the crest of her orgasm before Lucian was pulling out of her body. She made a sound of disappointment. "I swear, if you tease me, Lucian—"

He stood before her with his cock glistening wet and swollen and hard. *Definitely* ready for more. "On your hands and knees." His voice was hoarse with need.

A thrill coursed through her with the command in his voice. She scrambled to obey and was barely in position before he was slamming into her again. His groan was almost as satisfying as his cock... which somehow seemed to have grown larger. Or perhaps it was just the abandon with which he was burying it deep inside her. Or the magic sparking there. Or maybe even the pregnancy flushing her body with all kinds of heightened sensitivity. Whatever it was, she was already about to come again.

"God, Lucian!" she gasped, nearly pitching forward with how hard he was taking her. But his hands held her securely enough—she wasn't going anywhere but deep into Orgasm Land again.

His only response was more grunting and a more fevered pitch to his thrusting. She cried out as her orgasm pulsed around his cock, shuddering under the onslaught, sparking a pleasure that left her light-headed. As the aftershocks raced along her body, he kept thrusting. Then he groaned and pulled out. He climbed past her on the bed to sit at the head of it, his cock still glorious and tall and erect for her.

All for her.

Even though he'd already made her come twice, her mouth still watered at the sight of him.

He held out his hand to her. "Ride me," he commanded. "I want your body where I can reach it."

Another giddy flush of pleasure ran through her with his words. She climbed across the bed to him and lifted up on her knees. Getting in position required a bit of balancing with her belly between them, but with his help, she was soon sinking down on his shaft.

"Oh fuck, you're so tight," he groaned.

She loved that she brought him pleasure. That alone almost tripped her to the edge again. Instead, she started pumping, lifting then sinking on his gorgeously thick cock. He helped her along for a moment with hands on both her hips, then he slid one between her legs, flicking her nub.

"Oh God," she gasped. It was like electric shocks right on the verge of painful, they were so good. "Holy fuck." She pumped him faster.

"I know just what you like," he whispered, then dipped his head to lap at her breasts bouncing near his face. "Just what you need. Every bit of you belongs to me, and I'm going to pleasure you like no man ever has."

"You do that…" she panted as she bounced and impaled herself on his cock. "…every single time."

He grinned and slipped a hand to the back of her head, capturing her in a kiss that forced her to slow her frenetic pace. But the hand between her legs moved even faster, his magic-sparked fingertips delivering exquisite torture-pleasure.

"Oh, God, Lucian, yes, just like that, just like…" She was mumbling into his mouth, incoherent as the orgasm convulsed her again, ripping pleasure throughout her. Her body wracked against his, squeezing down on his cock as the rest of her lost the ability to hold herself up. He did it for her, holding her close, their baby-bump sandwiched between them as he wrenched aftershocks of pleasure out of her. When it had subsided a little, his grin was wide and self-satisfied.

"Three, by my count," he said, a wicked glint in his eye.

"You're counting?" she gasped, still not catching her breath.

"Oh yes." He slipped his hands to her hips. "But now it's my turn."

Oh God, yes. "How do you want me?" She would give this man everything and anything he asked.

"Lean back. Let me see your breasts bounce as I take you."

She did, although she wasn't sure she could hold that position—but she needn't have worried. He held her hip and the small of her back, supporting her… then he started thrusting up into her, deep and slow.

"So beautiful. So gorgeous. And all mine." It was like a mantra he was repeating to himself, not words for her, but they flushed pleasure through her anyway.

He picked up the pace, his cock sliding deep and rubbing against her nub on the way in.

"Oh! *Yes.* Don't stop," she breathed as she tipped her head back and lost herself in the slow, strong, and deep way he was making love to her.

"Never," he said, and it was a vow. But then he picked up the pace further, holding her fast with his hands as he thrust from below, piercing her body and soul with his pleasure-filled grunts and cries.

Just as he came, his hot seed spilling inside her, he let out a guttural groan that tipped her right over the edge again. They shook and ground together, endlessly drawing out the pleasure of their bodies.

Arabella was literally dizzy with their lovemaking.

She would need a rest, at least a few minutes.

Then she would go about pleasuring this man in all the ways she knew how. And any he cared to teach her. This gorgeous man had five hundred years of experience behind him, and she wanted to create five hundred more years of pleasure with him.

Now and forever.

Chapter Nine

LUCIAN HAD NEVER SEEN THE THRONE ROOM SO resplendent.

Then again, the House of Smoke had never received a True Angel before.

The dragons were restless, lining the edges of the throne room and waiting. Lucian stood stiffly at the front. His mother and father were seated on their thrones behind him, with his brothers flanking him on either side. Not that they expected any trouble from the angel, but even a halfling with an angel blade had the power to take out a dragon or demon or pretty much any supernatural creature. The powers of a True Angel were incomparably stronger. They were like the fae in that way—with powers both unknown and unknowable—and it wasn't the first time Lucian compared the two in his mind. They were bitter enemies—the angels mostly on the side of good, the fae chaotic and indifferent and conjurers of demons—but Lucian was convinced they shared a common ancestry of sorts. As if the fae had somehow devolved from angelic ancestors. Maybe they were a rogue branch of the Dark Angels, the shadow class, the ones who had fallen so far that they'd turned against their better natures and made common cause with the demonic forces of the world. The True Angels avoided all contact with demons. He wasn't sure what prevented them, but it seemed pretty absolute. Then again, Lucian didn't pretend to know how the angel realm functioned. With the exception of the occasional fallen angel bedding a human and producing angelings—who at least served a decent purpose in hunting down demons—True Angels kept themselves apart from humanity.

And that was all Lucian needed to know.

They apparently liked to keep dragons waiting as well.

The House of Smoke had been receiving guests all week—mostly dragons and witches and the occasional vampire, all coming to pledge their fealty or celebrate the impending renewal of the treaty.

Arabella was in the final week of her pregnancy, and he had her locked away in the other half of the keep, far from the busy traffic of the throne room and behind a heavy layer of wards on every side of his lair.

Not that he expected trouble. Not that he didn't have a legion of his best dragons, in case trouble decided to be unexpected. But simply because he would take no chances with his mate and his soon-to-be-born son, the next prince of the House of Smoke.

He half expected Zephan to make some last-ditch attempt to stop the birth of his son, even if it would violate the treaty and his own sworn, magical binding oath. Lucian wouldn't put it past the fae to find a way out of the magical shackles Zephan had voluntarily put on himself in exchange for his life.

A stirring at the back of the throne room near the door told him the angel must have arrived. Lucian would've reached out with his fae senses to confirm it, except reminding a True Angel of the fae blood running through his veins wasn't the smartest move. Lucian wanted to keep this calm, cool, and over as quickly as possible.

The doors to the throne room creaked as they

slowly drew open to reveal a male angel standing just outside.

A gasp went around the room.

The male had an unearthly beauty, even more so than the angelings Lucian had met before. He was taller than any normal human, and Lucian could already tell the angel would even tower over him. The angel's long, flowing brown hair lifted in some kind of magical breeze as he slowly stepped into the room, sweeping a gaze across the assembled dragons of Lucian's House. His broad white wings folded as he passed over the threshold and then expanded again to their full reach. The dragons stationed at the door flinched out of the way.

Lucian narrowed his eyes, scrutinizing this dramatic entrance. Was the angel just trying to demonstrate his power? Or was he simply as obtuse as every angeling Lucian had ever met?

The angel was nearly naked, dressed only in a filmy, nearly translucent toga over one shoulder that barely fell low enough to cover what ought to be covered when coming to a ceremony such as this. His ice-blue eyes blazed across the length of the room, and the raw power vibrating off him filled the air with a kind of electric hum. As he slowly strolled down the center, his wings folded once more behind him, this time disappearing into his back.

Erelah, the angeling who had captured Leksander's heart, trailed behind, her head held high with a gloriously beaming smile on her face.

"Markos likes to make an entrance," Leksander whispered at Lucian's side. There was more than a little hint of jealousy in his voice.

His brother had explained that Markos was an angel of the light, a Seraphim, protector class, and Erelah's faction leader. Ostensibly, that made him one of the good guys in the relative scheme of things. Now that Lucian had seen the angel himself, he hoped for Leksander's sake that the rumors were true—that Seraphim would occasionally fall for a human, given the love that all angels had for humanity, but they would never fuck one of their own angelings. It was some kind of taboo, although Lucian didn't really understand why. Erelah was the product of just such a union between a human mother and a Seraphim father, so clearly fucking humans was acceptable. Why not angelings, who were at least part angel? Did they not have sex with *each other?* Maybe that was the taboo part.

Lucian didn't understand angels, period.

But he knew Markos *wasn't* Erelah's father. And

with the way she was looking at him—a look that was as close to lust as Lucian had ever seen on her face—Markos could have her in his bed with barely a nod. Leksander claimed only shadow class angels thought it proper to sleep with their own hybrid creatures, and protector class angels like Markos would never stoop so low. Lucian cared only in not wanting his brother's heart ground into the dirt—by this angel or the gorgeous angeling by his side.

The slow, majestic, and largely arrogant walk that Markos took down the long length of throne room finally brought him face-to-face with Lucian.

He was right—Markos towered over him. The angel was almost too large to be confused for human. He would have to stow his wings and use some kind of glamour to hide his unearthly beauty in order to pass, and even then… the hum of power coming off him would trigger suspicion. Then again, Lucian suspected any human female would be as happy to fall in Markos's bed as Erelah appeared to be.

"Welcome to the House of Smoke," Lucian said, spreading his arms wide and not so incidentally turning his palms toward the angel, displaying his fae runes which were jumping about frenetically across his skin in response to the nearness of all that angelic power.

Markos didn't answer, just glanced to the side as Erelah skirted around him. She wore a similar toga —it barely covering her ample curves and appeared to be held on with thin, golden strings across the sides. She cupped a small box in her hands that seemed made out of pure energy. More white glow than container, it had just enough solidity to convince Lucian it was real.

"A gift for the new prince," Erelah said, ducking her head and holding the box up high, cradled in her open palms.

Lucian wasn't sure if he should take it—not just because the protocol here was completely unprecedented, but also because angel-imbued items had at least the possibility of being deadly for dragons.

"This will not harm you, Lucian Smoke, prince of the House of Smoke," Markos said, his voice booming. It was overly loud, almost in angel mode, and Lucian had to steel himself against cowering away from it.

The angel tipped his head. "My apologies." His voice was considerably dimmer now, but still vibrating with power. "I'm not accustomed to traveling in your realm."

"We appreciate your visit and your gift," Lucian said carefully. "It is unexpected, yet welcome."

Erelah's face still beamed, but Lucian could see the smile wearing a little at the edges. He had not yet taken the box. He reached out a hand, and the fae runes scurried away from the tips of his fingers as he took the gift from her.

"Should I ask what it is?" Lucian directed his question with no small amount of humor at Erelah.

Her eyes went wide, and she flicked her gaze back and forth between Markos and Lucian as if she were afraid to speak out of turn.

Lucian sighed and turned back to Markos. "If there are any precautions I should take with this gift, perhaps you can tell me now."

The power that radiated from Markos's face dimmed a little—it made Lucian think of a cloud blocking the sun, and he shuddered a little with it. "There is nothing wrong with the gift." Some of the booming angelvoice had come back, and this time, Lucian did flinch, if only slightly.

"No offense intended." He drew his words out slowly and clearly. Pissing off an angel was not how he wanted this to go, and it wasn't as if angels and dragons were natural friends to start with.

The war in heaven that created the fallen angels

had divided them into light and dark, and if the stories could be believed, Lucifer, the highest of the archangels, took the form of a dragon in his fight against the archangel Michael. Lucifer was now in shadow, but all the light class angels—the Seraphim, the archangels, and even the more nebulous aeons—still didn't much care for the dragon form. Or the fae magic that churned through Lucian's veins.

Markos's ice blue eyes were trained on him, piercing, and Lucian had no doubt that if he had a soul that Markos was taking its inventory as they spoke.

After a moment, the angel said, "The box carries a blessing. It is meant for the child. No other shall use it."

A small shiver went through Lucian. He didn't want to think about what would happen if the blessing was somehow bestowed upon someone it was not intended for.

He tipped his head. "Thank you. It is a generous gift." He handed it off to Leksander at his side, whose eyes were as wide as Erelah's. Lucian felt like he was handing him a live grenade. Hopefully, Erelah would have some guidance on how to appropriately use it. Or dispose of it. Lucian wasn't sure he even wanted it in the House, much less actually use it on his unborn child. But none of that would keep him from graciously thanking the angel for his gift… and hoping he would leave. Soon.

Especially given that the Queen of the Summer Court was due to make her appearance in just a short while. Another historic visit for the soon-to-be-born prince of the House of Smoke. Whereas Zephan from the Winter Court had made several unwelcome advances, the Summer Court always kept their distance from the House of Smoke. And while the Winter Court might loathe dragons and humanity in general, the Summer Court had particular ill feelings left over from the time the original treaty had been brokered, and the magical love spell behind it created. They had not soon forgotten that a dragon had seduced their queen and formed the bloodline that would be propagated for twelve thousand years… and one more generation with the birth of Lucian's son.

He was relishing the Summer Queen's visit even less than the appearance of this Seraphim before him.

Markos spread his hands wide, palms forward in blessing. His wings unfurled behind him.

Lucian leaned back and tensed.

"A blessing upon the protectors of humanity." Marcus's voice boomed in full angel mode. A flush of magic pulsed through Lucian, and by the gasp that went around the room, everyone else received the "blessing" as well.

And then, in half a blink, Markos was gone.

Leksander still stood by his side, holding the blessing box rigidly in his hands.

Leonidas on his other side let out a low whistle. "I'm glad that's over," he said, wryly. "No offense, Erelah."

Her whole body had relaxed from the vibrant joy that had been emanating from it before, but a dreamy smile remained on her face.

"You all right?" It was Leksander asking, but Lucian wasn't the only one who could hear the sharp edge of jealousy in his voice. Leonidas raised an eyebrow and cocked his head towards Erelah, expectant.

She didn't seem to notice, but she did blink her way out of her infatuated daydreaming, or whatever was preoccupying her. She gave Lucian a fervent look, striding over to grab hold of his hands and squeeze. "You have a blessing from a True Angel for your child!" she gushed.

Leksander grimaced at the box in his hands.

"Erelah, what do I do with this? I will admit to not wanting to hold it any longer than necessary."

"Of course, not!" she scolded. "It's not meant for you." She strode over and gently, reverently lifted it from Leksander's hands and cradled it to her chest. Then she closed her eyes and let out a sigh that made Leksander's eyes grow cold.

"Perhaps you could deliver it," Lucian hurried out, before his brother's heart could be eviscerated any further. "I'm sure Arabella wouldn't mind a visit, especially for the delivery of such a..." He flicked a look of warning at Leksander. "...*powerful* gift."

"That is a perfect idea!" Erelah whirled around, her diaphanous dress billowing out as she turned, revealing more of her curves than she probably intended.

Lucian could see his brother soften at the sight, no doubt yearning for her as he always did. But after meeting a True Angel in the flesh—so to speak, given they weren't really human at all— Lucian was convinced more than ever that his brother's quest to win this angeling's heart was thoroughly doomed. Not when a Seraphim left her dizzy and swooning. How could a dragon even compete with that?

"Well, after this delightful encounter," Leonidas said, breaking the tension, "meeting the Summer Queen should be a breeze."

Lucian shook his head.

He would be glad when the receiving of gifts and the formal ceremonies were behind him, and he could return once again to his lair, his mate, and very soon... *his child.*

Chapter Ten

ONLY FIVE MORE DAYS, AND ARABELLA WOULD BE A *mama.*

The idea thrilled and terrified her—what the hell did she know about being a mom?—and yet somehow, impossibly, it looked like it might really happen. The last few weeks, ever since she'd had that horrible hot flash that almost took her and the baby, she'd been fine. Perfect. Blissful even, except for the increasingly awkward belly that was just ridiculous at this point. She couldn't even *see her feet!* She glanced down to check, and nope—her bare toes weren't even close to visible over the basketball-sized belly she was sporting. She'd given up wearing shoes because she never left the lair, so seriously, what was the point? Her full-time job was now eating enough to keep up with the baby, professional-level napping, and being the recipient of multiple orgasms courtesy of Lucian. Their love-making had hardly slowed down, even as the baby grew, and Lucian insisted on finding new ways to make her come every day.

She wasn't complaining about that part. Or any of it, really.

She shoved another spoonful of mint chocolate chip ice cream in her mouth and tried not to think about how spoiled—and dependent on everyone else—she had become in such a short time.

Rachel scowled at the heap of presents, half still wrapped, in the corner of the nursery. "What in the world are we supposed to do with all this stuff?" she complained, hands on hips. Then she dug into the pile.

The gifts had been flowing in, non-stop for weeks, and they'd just been piling up in the corner until Arabella figured out what she was supposed to do with it all. Literally none of it was practical—between the magic and the money of her billion-aire-dragon-shifter mate, this baby would want for nothing. The gifts came from all over the immortal world and were entirely symbolic or just weird stuff she had no idea what it even meant. But now that the baby was just days away, it was time to clear out the clutter. Rachel attacked the problem with the efficiency she normally brought to their business, which had been sadly neglected while they were holed up in the mountains, trying to make sure Arabella and the baby both *lived*.

But once the baby was born, what then? Would she really be able to go back to the office?

Arabella couldn't even think that far ahead. All of her energy was absorbed in growing the tiny, feisty little guy in her belly. As if on cue, he churned around inside there. She patted him absently, stroking whatever fist or tiny foot he was poking her with this time. He quickly settled down.

Rachel backed out of the pile and held up something metallic for inspection. "I know the immortal world has some crazy fetish for the impractical, but this gift, though?" It looked like a tiny chainmail blanket. "Seriously… why?"

"To keep baby dragons warm?"

"Wait… what?" Rachel straightened. "Are you saying the baby will shift into a dragon? Like a little dragon? A tiny, crazy, fire-breathing, midget dragon?"

"Mm-hmm," Arabella said around her mouthful of ice cream. Then she licked the spoon clean and wistfully set the bowl down on the dresser that was fully-stocked with tiny clothes for a tiny human/dragon shifter baby. "Lucian says dragons can shift even in the womb. It's #541 on the list of Things Lucian Worries Might Go Wrong."

Rachel's nose scrunched up. "Is he seriously telling you all those things? What's wrong with that man?"

"Absolutely nothing." Arabella sighed, thinking about the last time they'd made love—just that morning before he'd gotten all dressed up and gone off for another round of meeting important people in the immortal world, all come to congratulate him on the impending birth of his son. She missed him when he was gone—a high-pitched aching kind of feeling that wasn't at all comfortable and that required lots of Reconnection Sex as soon as they got back together again—but she was happy to avoid the official ceremonies. She was out of her element there.

Who was she kidding? She was out of her element in *all* of this. But sorting through gifts with Rachel was a pretty decent way to keep her mind off the impending mama-hood.

Not to mention the birth itself, which sort of terrified her.

Rachel was shaking her head and draping the chainmail blankie over the side of the crib. "I'm glad you're smitten by Hottie McPrince." She gestured to Arabella's belly. "Makes for good baby-making." She nodded in approval. "But no man's that perfect. I think he's yanking your chain about this baby-flying-dragon thing."

"It would be pretty damn cute, tho," Arabella pointed out.

"Yeah… until he set the drapes on fire."

Arabella tilted her head, conceding the point. She had no idea how to raise a dragonling—she was still working on just growing one, and that was pretty much automatic. It was a good thing there was a whole House full of dragons who would help with that job.

The nursery had been completely redecorated by now into a very modern-looking baby room, complete with colorful animals on the walls and light-blocking drapes on the windows. A border edged the walls where they met the ceiling comprised of ancient-looking letters, the same kind Lucian had on his skin—he said they were wards to protect the baby. The entire lair had all sorts of wards on it, Lucian reassured her, although those were invisible. But that was part of why she never left the lair now—not when they were so close to having the baby arrive.

Arabella rubbed her belly as the baby kicked again. "When the baby gets here, we should just put Cinaed on baby-watching duty." She smirked. "He's already on Arabella-watching duty twenty-four-seven. I'm sure he'd be happy to watch the baby while you and I get back to work."

Rachel stopped unwrapping the silver crinkly paper of the latest package and gave Arabella a serious look. "Are you going back to work, Ari?"

Arabella frowned. "The office needs me. But to be honest…"

Rachel put down the box and came to stand by her. She eyed Arabella's belly. "You want to stay with him, don't you?"

Arabella rested her hand on the top of the mound that was her son. "Yeah, I do. But there are a lot of women who need our help, Rach—how do I just say no to that? I mean, after the baby is born? After all, once that's settled, once the baby survives, the treaty is fulfilled. There's nothing that says I have to take care of him full-time by myself."

Rachel rolled her eyes. "As if you would be taking care of him by yourself anyway!" She flicked a hand back to the pile of gifts. "As far as I can tell, this is going to be the most spoiled baby in the history of babies."

Arabella smiled. "You're right about that. And none of these dragons have jobs—they're all independently wealthy. Surely one of them can watch the baby for a while."

"I think you're going to have to fight them off just to have the baby to yourself for a few minutes." Rachel shook her head like she didn't understand how the baby madness could've infected so many hulking grown men, but there was no question about it. There had been a steady stream of visitors coming through to see Arabella and her baby belly. She suspected half the gifts were just an excuse to visit and ooh and ahhh over the fact that she was pregnant. She couldn't even imagine what it would be like when the baby had actually arrived.

"You're right," Arabella said. "This baby is going to have more caretakers than he knows what to do with." She couldn't help the wistfulness in her voice. This baby was *her* baby… and Lucian's. She wanted to be the one to hold him and cuddle him and kissed him and shower him with all the love that she felt bursting in her heart already before he was even born.

"But *you're* his mama," Rachel said softly.

"Crazy, right? What do I know about being a mom?" Suddenly, there were tears threatening the corners of her eyes, and she wiped angrily at them. She'd been doing way too much of that, lately—her eyes were like a crazy bucket of tears just waiting to overflow at the slightest little thing. Damn dragon pregnancy hormones. But the feeling was real— Arabella had grown up in a series of foster homes, just like Rachel. Neither one of them had anything that really resembled a mother. Everyone was just passing through.

Rachel grasped hold of her hand and squeezed it. "You're going to be the best damn mama ever!"

Arabella hiccupped through a little laugh.

But Rachel's expression was serious. "If you want to have that baby all to yourself," she said fiercely, "you do just that. You risked your life to have this child. *You* get to decide how much time to spend with him. And don't worry about the office— besides, I found a paralegal that's been holding down the fort for us in Seattle. I've been working with her on the side."

"You have?" Arabella drew back and gave her a suspicious look. Rachel didn't keep secrets from her, not usually. "When were you going to tell me about this?"

"You've had your hands full," she said, waving at the tower of sparkly packages and the miniature crib set up in the middle of the room. It was carved from some ancient kind of wood, and Lucian said it had been in his family for generations. Which, given how long dragons lived, meant the crib had to be thousands of years old. He'd given it a new coat of varnish or something because it looked weathered but beautiful. And soon she would be putting their child to sleep in it.

She really didn't want to miss a minute of that.

Arabella nodded slowly and looked back to her best friend. "Thank you, Rach. I feel like I should say that about a thousand times for all the help you're giving me."

Now Rachel's eyes were glassy with tears. She leaned over Arabella's belly and put her arms around her neck and gave her a squeeze. "What are sisters for, if not this kind of shit?"

Arabella laughed and hugged her back. Then she released her. "Okay, I'm only going back to work if that's what *I* want to do—not because I have to keep the office going. Because we'll figure out a way to help all our clients even if I'm on Mama Duty. Deal?"

"Deal." Rachel scowled at the pile of presents.

"I suppose just tossing these out the window isn't acceptable?"

"Probably not."

Just as Rachel dove back into the pile, the door to the nursery swung open.

Cinaed's smiling face poked in. "Is my lady up to having a visitor?"

"Another one?" She honestly had thought they were done with that—seemed like every dragon in the House had come through.

"This one bears a special gift from the angels," Cinaed said solemnly. "But if my lady is not fit for receiving guests, I will send her on her way, angeling or no." The resolution on Cinaed's face was absolute—Arabella was certain he would turn away the king himself if Arabella wasn't up for it.

"Angeling?" Rachel asked, turning away from the pile of gifts with a frown on her face.

"Is it Erelah?" Arabella asked him. He nodded. "Well, let her in. She's practically an auntie to this baby!"

Rachel muttered something about angelings for aunties and went back to excavating the pile. "Last time, that girl brought a knife. For a baby." She sorted through the pile and came up with the angel blade. "I'm no expert on kids, but even I know that a baby doesn't need a knife."

Arabella just smiled. "I'm glad you found it. I've been meaning to mount that on the wall or something."

"On the wall?" Rachel gave her a look like she was crazy and set it carefully on top of the dresser like she didn't want to hold it any longer than necessary.

Before Arabella could answer, the door swung open again, and Erelah breezed in, carrying a glowing white box resting in the palms of both her hands. Cinaed trailed behind.

"Erelah!" Arabella exclaimed with genuine warmth. "How are you?"

But Erelah didn't reply, just bent down on one knee and held the box up to her. "I bring you a blessing straight from the Seraphim Markos," she said solemnly, with a resonance in her voice that seemed to shake the walls.

"Um... okay." Arabella stared at the box, not quite sure what to do—it was glowing white and pulsing a little and seemed entirely too filled with energy for her to touch it.

Cinaed was looking likewise concerned,

hovering nearby like he planned to snatch the box away if Arabella reached for it. "Careful, my lady."

"What do I do with it, Erelah?" she asked, cautiously.

The angeling looked up at her, eyes shining. "Why, all you have to do is accept it. *Believe* in it— you already have the power of True Love. Your belief is already a tremendous force. All you must do is reach for it."

Arabella bit her lip and gave Cinaed a sideways look.

He was frowning. "My lord wouldn't have sent it, I suppose, if it weren't safe."

If there was one thing Arabella trusted, it was Lucian's desire keep her and the baby safe. She reached for the box, and when she touched it, a white light flared and washed over her. It was a gentle breeze filled with magic, energizing and enervating her entire body. The baby stirred and jumped, and her hand went reflexively to her belly.

Cinaed's alarm jumped five levels. "My lady! Are you all right?"

The blessing was still filling her with a joyful glow as if the light of the box were pouring liquid happiness into her. "Cinaed, I'm fine. Wonderful, in fact." She struggled for the right word to describe the feeling, but then it flowed from her lips. "I am blessed." She smiled down at Erelah, who then jumped to her feet. The angeling seemed like she wanted to embrace Arabella, but was holding back. So Arabella went to her, throwing her arms around the barely-clad woman. She could feel the power surging through Erelah's body just with that simple contact.

When she pulled back, Erelah's eyes were shining even brighter. "You are truly blessed," she gushed.

The baby kicked especially hard with the angeling's nearness. Cinaed's attention was drawn to her belly, and he seemed transfixed as a little ripple of movement moved from one side to the other.

Then he looked sharply to Erelah. "My lady grows tired. It is best that you leave."

Arabella didn't want him to shoo her away, but the aftermath of the blessing *was* leaving her a little tired.

"Of course." Erelah's smile didn't dim in the slightest. She dipped her head and then quickly turned to leave. Cinaed watched her go but didn't follow. Then he came closer to Arabella's side, still transfixed by her belly.

"The little prince is active?" He seemed intensely curious about it.

"It's hard to say what sets him off," Arabella said with a small smile. "But all kinds of magic seem to get him jazzed up." She snuck a look at Rachel to see what she made of Cinaed's fascination. She was just shaking her head.

"What does it feel like?" he asked, and his eyes popped a little wider as the baby did his rolling motion again, sending a little bump traveling across the span of Arabella's belly. "May I…" He reached halfway to her belly, then stopped, looking uncertain.

Arabella grinned and took his hand, pulling it the rest of the way and laying it flat against her t-shirt covered belly. Cinaed dropped to his knees, bringing his face close to his hand and watching wide-eyed.

"It's just a baby," Rachel called from across the room, scowling.

He threw her a quick frown. "It is a *miracle*. And a prince. And—" He cut off and whipped his gaze back as the baby moved again, under his hand this time. He seemed speechless for a moment, then he said, "It's a wonder, my lady."

She laughed lightly. "What's a wonder is how

much mint chocolate chip ice cream this baby requires. I think I'm out, Cinaed."

He looked panicked and leaped to his feet. "I'll get more right away!" Then he fled out the door.

"You really shouldn't do that to him," Rachel said with a frown.

"I think he's super cute around the baby." Arabella stuck her tongue out at her.

"He's *super hot*—there's a difference."

But Arabella could tell her best friend was affected by the sight of this super-gorgeous man kneeling in front of Arabella's belly and oohing and awwing over her baby. Rachel could hide it all she wanted, but Arabella could see it—she had feelings for Cinaed and not just the lust kind.

"Well, undeniable super hotness *is* how it starts…" Arabella arched an eyebrow at her.

"Don't get on that again!" Rachel scowled and picked up the angel blade off the dresser. "Alright, what do you want to do with this?"

"I told you—on the wall. Maybe over the crib."

"Okay, fine." Rachel walked over to the wall and held it up, eyeing where it might be best to mount it.

"That looks good," Arabella said. "But you're not getting out of talking about Cinaed."

"There's nothing to talk about." Rachel set the blade back on the dresser next to the crib. "He's super hot. And possibly super cute when he's taking care of you and the baby." She crossed her arms and gave Arabella a determined look. "And it's obvious he's the kind of dragon who wants all that stuff—True Love and a dragonling. I'm just not the kind of girl for that sort of thing."

Arabella gave her best friend a long look. "You could be, Rach. Look at me." She gestured to her oversized belly. "I'm about to fulfill an ancient treaty by bearing a dragon shifter baby. That wasn't exactly in my five-year plan."

Rachel arched an eyebrow. "You had a five-year plan?"

"Always." She gave her best friend a very serious look. "Rachel, this is the best thing that's ever happened to me. Lucian is the kind of man I never even knew existed. I fell in love with him because I'd literally never believed anyone could be that good... until I met him. Give it a chance, Rach. I want all that for you."

Rachel's mouth was working, but no words are coming out. Finally, she looked away and pounded her fist lightly on the top of the dresser. "Why do you have to look so damn happy when you say that?"

Arabella smiled. "I just received an angel blessing for my dragon baby. I think this smile is going to be plastered on my face for a while."

Rachel snorted a laugh. "Okay, well, that's your life. Always been better at it than I have been, Ari. You had to rescue me off the streets, not the other way around—remember?" She met Arabella's gaze. "I'm not the kind of woman a man like Cinaed stays with."

Arabella trundled across the span of the room to take her friend by the shoulders and stare her in the eyes. "Don't you talk smack about my best friend. She dropped everything to take care of me and my baby. She's *awesome*. And I don't want to hear anyone say anything else—including you."

Rachel smiled through the tears. "You have to love me. You're my sister."

"No, I don't—but I do." She gently squeezed Rachel's shoulders. "You are exactly the kind of woman a man like Cinaed falls in love with. Let it happen, Rach. Don't fight it."

Rachel swiped away the tears from her eyes. "Now you sound like that horny voice in my head that wants to jump his bones whenever he walks into the room."

Arabella grinned and released her. "That's what I'm talking about. I don't know how you've resisted him this long, to be honest."

But Rachel just shook her head. "I've got things to do other than chasing after hot dragons." She pulled away and eyed the pile of packages. "These gifts aren't going to unwrap themselves." And with that, her friend stalked back to the pile and dug into it again.

But Rachel was right—Arabella had to focus on getting the baby here. Once that was accomplished —once Arabella had all of her dreams come true, even the ones she hadn't known she had—she was going to make sure Rachel's came true as well.

Chapter Eleven

LUCIAN HAD ENOUGH OF CEREMONY TO LAST HIM the rest of his five hundred years.

Assuming the magic of his dragonling son's birth actually occurred.

Lucian watched as the House of Fyre filed out after depositing their gifts—sacks of gold. Traditional dragon gifts, to be sure, but nothing special. Lucian was just glad Cinaed missed the parade of assholes that was his former House. Lucian hadn't realized they were coming until they showed up at the perimeter station. It was the House of Smoke's front door, where every immortal had to stop first and ask for the wards to be dropped so they could gain entrance to the keep. Lucian had been reluctant to permit the House of Fyre entry, but his mother and father convinced him that repairing old wounds was more important. And that historic occasions such as the birth of his son and the renewal the treaty practically demanded it.

Lucian still didn't like it.

As it was, the House of Fyre made their visit perfunctory and short—which worked well, considering the Summer Court Queen was waiting with arrogant impatience at perimeter station. The House of Fyre was leaving just in time.

"That went rather well," Leonidas said, adjusting the cuffs on his jacket. "Let us pray to all that's magic that the Summer Queen is likewise terse in her congratulations."

His brother was chafing under his formal attire. The ceremonies were keeping him from whichever female he had seduced lately and left languishing in his lair. Lucian didn't begrudge him the desire to be elsewhere—he felt it, too. And Leksander had been in an outright dark mood ever since Erelah and her Seraphim faction leader, Markos, had made their appearance. It was getting insufferable to be in the same room with him.

Leksander spoke into his phone, whispering soft commands to the dragons guarding the royal entrance just off the throne room. They had divided the House of Smoke in two, with separate wards protecting each. That way, only the half with the throne room had wards dropping and rising with every visitor that came to call.

Mostly, it was just dragons.

But the fae were unpredictable, and if anything, the Summer Court had more reason to hate Lucian and the House of Smoke than the Winter Court. The magic of his blood bound them to an ancient treaty that reminded them of the betrayal of the past. And those past times weren't so distant for the fae, given they lived far longer than Lucian's five hundred or a thousand years, depending on whether his dragonling survived. The current Queen of the Summer Court was a direct descendent of the original queen whose life and love forged the magical bond that undergird the treaty—and whose blood ran through Lucian's veins. The original queen was ten generations back for Lucian, but only one for Nyssa, the pure-blooded fae daughter who was born before the queen's liaison with the dragon she fell in love with. Nyssa was one of the original aggrieved offspring; Lucian and his brothers and his mother and father were the bastard children who had snarled up fae politics for the last twelve thousand years.

And in all those twelve thousand years, no summer fae had visited the House of Smoke. Not for the birth of a new generation or any other purpose. Speculation was rampant as to the cause, but Lucian suspected it was merely the fact that the Winter Court had been making a habit of interfering with the House of Smoke's lineage. The rivalry between Winter and Summer was strong— and it had to tweak Nyssa that Zephan had such an influence over affairs that affected her court as well.

Leksander finished speaking into his phone and gave Lucian a nod.

Lucian straightened and faced down the length of the throne room.

Just as with the Seraphim, the door opened before the queen made her entrance. He had heard tell of her beauty—all the fae were spectacularly beautiful—but he was unprepared for the ethereal quality of it. Her hair was white—not the snow white of someone advancing in age, but the unearthly silver-white of a woman who has chosen the color precisely. The curls were piled on top of her head and fell down the back of her silver-and-white ruffled dress, which swept the floor behind her, floating in some kind of magical wind as she glided down the cleared aisle. Dragons on either side leaned back, and even Lucian could feel the power emanating from her. Zephan, a prince of the Winter Court, had powers he chose to flick Lucian's way when they fought, but this was altogether something different. Strings of silver decorated the open neck of her dress, sparkling and flittering lightly as the queen took her time strolling to the front. As she drew closer, Lucian could see her nearly-clear eyes were rimmed with violet.

"Cousin," she greeted him. For all her cool, unearthly beauty and color, her voice was warm, more so than the winter fae and their affinity for coldness and dark.

Lucian restrained a reflexive smile. He didn't make the mistake of assuming he could use the same familiarity. "Your highness." He dipped his head in greeting.

"I hear you have a child in waiting," she said.

"We appreciate your visit," Lucian said carefully. His runes were dancing along his skin and managed to climb his neck, enlivened by the nearness of their queen. He was *dragon*, and his allegiance was forever with the House of Smoke, but the magic in his veins knew no boundaries, and it recognized the fae of its origin.

The queen raised a dark, pencil-thin eyebrow at the movement of his runes showing above his formal attire. "I wish to see for myself this woman who would bear the next generation of the House of Smoke."

Lucian's heart seized, but he kept his expression cool. He flicked a look to Leonidas—his brother's face had gone blank, no doubt steeling against the rage that the fae queen would even suggest such a thing.

"I'm afraid my mate is indisposed at the moment," Lucian said, slowly and measuring out each word. He could feel the tension mounting throughout the throne room. "She is but days away from delivery."

Nyssa gave him a barely perceptible nod and let her gaze travel for the first time around the room, taking in his brothers, his mother and father seated on their thrones behind him, and the dragons standing now at hyper-alert attention behind her. Lucian had no doubt that she could, with a flick of her wrist, bat them away. But even if she wished to make her own unescorted trip to the other side of the keep to where Arabella was safely tucked in his lair, Nyssa would not be able to get past the wards they had erected.

At least, he hoped.

"I sense that she is well-loved and well-protected," Nyssa said coolly. "As it should be for someone who has to fulfill a treaty with True Love."

Lucian frowned, unsure whether that was meant in sarcasm or not. The summer fae were as inscrutable as the winter fae. But her meaning was unimportant as long as she didn't make a move against them.

Nyssa held up a hand, and with a slight tremor of her fingers, a tiny bronze dragon appeared in her palm. She held it out to Lucian, and he cautiously stepped forward to take the gift from her. His heart hammered. Gifts from fae—not something he actually wanted to keep inside his home, much less close to his child.

"Thank you." He stepped back.

Leonidas was scowling at the tiny dragon, but holding his tongue—Leonidas himself was a bronze dragon. Was there some kind of significance to that? But it wasn't his place to say anything. As the crown prince, Lucian spoke for the House, but he wasn't sure what he could say that would be of help in the situation.

"It is merely a dragon," Nyssa said with the faint trace of a smile—one that actually enhanced her beauty even more and somehow softened it. "Although it possesses the ability to soothe a child. We so rarely have children at Court, I am not familiar with how they behave. But I hear that children cry. Inexplicably. The token should alleviate that."

"A thoughtful gift, indeed." Lucian made a mental note to dispose of it as quickly as possible.

Nyssa tipped her head as if it were a genuine compliment. Then she turned, a graceful pirouette that preceded her slow glide back toward the door. But she only went two steps before stopping and throwing a glance back over her shoulder. "Cousin, take care. There is more to this birth than you know. The immortal world is watching."

Lucian scowled and opened his mouth to ask what the hell she meant by that, but she turned her back on him and slowly strode down the throne room. He decided to let it go.

When she reached the doorway, she made her own exit. With the wards temporarily down, she was able to use a fae doorway to her realm, where in the Summer and Winter Courts existed. The doorway was literally a rip in the fabric of space and time that she simply glided through with her silver-white hair and flowing dress.

As soon as she was gone, Leonidas spoke up. "You're absolutely forbidden from letting that dragon anywhere near my nephew."

"Agreed," Leksander said, coming up to stand next to Leonidas and Lucian at the front of the throne room. "I do not wish to guess what manner of spell she has put on this token."

Lucian nodded and handed it over to Leksander. "Maybe your angelfire girl can find a good way to dispose of it. One that won't have the magic backlashing on us."

He agreed with a sharp nod, but the dark look that had temporarily lifted from Leksander's face settled on it again.

Leonidas scowled. "What did Nyssa mean by there being more to the birth than we know? I don't like the sound of that."

"Neither do I." Lucian grimaced, but he'd had enough of the immortal world for the day. All he wanted was to get back to Arabella and his son and reassure himself that they were both still all right.

He raised his hands to the gathered dragons from his House, all getting a bit restless after the fae queen had made her exit. "You've all been extraordinarily patient throughout this time of formalities." His voice carried and quieted the crowd. "I appreciate your fealty even more now than ever. But I believe we're done dealing with royal matters now." He threw a smile back to his mother and father. His mother was beaming at him, but his father looked like he had just been startled awake. Lucian held in his laugh and turned back to the House. "I think we could all use a rest."

A twitter of laughter went through the crowd. The House had great affection for King Larik, but they knew he was nearing the end of his thousand years. And there was a bittersweetness that the arrival of his son would mean that his father and mother were probably in the final year of their lives. The House knew it as well. They were gentle with his mother and father in all things, another thing that earned his love for his fellow dragons. "Be well, my friends. The next time you see me, I hope to have a dragonling in my arms."

A roar of approval went up, and applause broke out with some whooping and hollering. It brought a broad smile to Lucian's face, and Leonidas clapped a hand on his shoulder, smiling wide as well. Lucian turned and hugged his brother, fiercely. Not only would he lose his mother and father in the next year, but his unmated brothers would likely go to wyvern as well. He was gaining everything—a mate and a child—and losing everything at the same time. The fatigue of the proceedings and the bitter sweetness of it washed over him.

Definitely time to get back to his lair—and rejuvenate in love again.

Dragons were drifting throughout the hall, muttering and laughing and chattering up a storm. Above all the noise, Lucian heard one word jump out and stab into him.

"What?" It was Leksander shouting his disbelief into his phone. "You've got to be kidding me."

Lucian flicked a look to Leonidas, and they both strode quickly over to where Leksander stood off to the side of the thrones.

"What is it?" Lucian asked.

"Get up here *immediately*," Leksander growled into the phone. Then he slapped it off and gritted his teeth. "Tytus is here from the House of Drakkon."

"You mean here at the perimeter station," Lucian said, his heart squeezing. The black dragon had already kidnapped his mate once—Lucian sure as hell wasn't going to give him another chance.

"I mean here at the *keep*," Leksander spat.

"What the fuck, Leksander?" Leonidas bit out.

"I know," Leksander said. "Somehow, the wards were still left down from when Nyssa was leaving. They were expecting her, but Tytus arrived instead."

"So, he just skips through the perimeter, and now he's knocking at our door?" Lucian's rage was reaching a boiling point.

"He's on his way to the throne room." Leksander held up his hands. "I've got a guard on him. He's alone. He's not a danger, Lucian."

"The hell he's not," Lucian said, dashing a look to the throne room door.

"What the fuck is he doing here?" Leonidas asked, the horror on his face matching Lucian's.

Leksander jerked his chin toward the door to the throne room. "Ask him yourself." The door had been left open by the fae queen's departure, and already Tytus was strolling through it, the dark smirk on his face making Lucian's skin crawl.

"I vowed to kill that dragon if I ever saw him again," Lucian said, but Leksander's hand was on his shoulder, holding him back.

"Maybe he's here to make amends," Leksander whispered hoarsely. "You're about to renew the treaty, Lucian. Let him give his gift and be on his way. You don't need a House war on the eve of the birth of your child."

Lucian growled, but Leksander was right.

Dragon heads were whipping to follow Tytus's quick-strided march down the throne room. Several half-shifted like they wanted to go after him, held back only by the fact that Lucian himself was unmoving, awaiting Tytus's approach. All eyes were on the two of them, watching to see who would make the first move. Lucian could take Tytus in a fight, easily and by himself—his fae magic would overpower a mere black dragon. And with his House surrounding Tytus, there was hardly any threat to letting the man have his ugly say, whatever it was.

Lucian made no promises about accepting any actual gifts.

Tytus smiled wide as if they were old friends. "Lucian Smoke of the House of Smoke. So I hear you're going to be a daddy." The smirk on his face was so irritating, Lucian couldn't help the growl that worked its way out of his chest.

"Whatever you have to say, Tytus, get it over with. And get the hell out of my House."

Tytus nodded and looked around casually. "So

this is what the House of Smoke looks like on the inside. A little ostentatious, if you ask me."

"Precisely no one is asking you," Lucian spat.

Tytus dipped his head in deference and spread his arms wide with a slight bow. "Of course. The last time we met was under rather... *extreme* circumstances."

"The last time we met, you kidnapped my mate and gave her to the fae." Just saying the words was making Lucian's runes writhe and twitch to lash out their magic at him. "If you think I'm going to forgive that—"

Tytus give an elaborate shrug. "That's just the problem, don't you see? I shouldn't need your forgiveness for taking something so easily snatched."

Lucian surged forward, but Leksander's grip on his shoulder held him back.

Leonidas stepped in front of Lucian. "Do you have a death wish, dragon?" he asked of Tytus. "Because there are plenty of dragons in this room who would be happy to grant it."

But Tytus just smirked. "The House of Smoke is filled with bravery when they outnumber you a hundred to one. But that only covers up the weak-willed nature of their chosen leaders. The princes of the House of Smoke have fae blood in their veins..." His face twisted with a look of disgust. "Without that and the protection of the treaty, you'd all be powerless against the combined forces of the rest of the dragon Houses. If you think I don't speak the truth about this, you know not what is happening in your own realm."

Leonidas frowned and flicked a look to Lucian. The same doubt was turning through Lucian's mind—*what the hell was Tytus talking about?*

The black dragon spread his arms wide and grinned. "And now the high and mighty prince has finally spawned a dragonling. Just days away now, so I hear. Which is really unfortunate, because it is long past the time that the treaty should have been broken."

Lucian narrowed his eyes. "Zephan sent you here, didn't he?"

"I don't need a fae to tell me what needs to be done." Tytus's eyes glittered dark. "It's obvious to anyone with eyes to see."

Leonidas gave Lucian another concerned look. Leksander's grip on his shoulder released as his phone chirped at him. He pressed it to his ear and frowned.

Lucian turned back to Tytus. "The treaty *will* be renewed," he ground out. "You can take your madness and pedal it elsewhere. Get out of my House. *Now.*"

Tytus held his hands up in surrender. "There's just one thing," he said, a smirk tugging at his lips. "I'm not the one who needs to leave."

What? Just as Lucian was coming to the conclusion that Tytus had lost his mind, and Lucian might have to actually kill him—

"What the hell—" Leksander's face held an ocean of shock.

A spear of panic shot through Lucian's chest.

Leksander's eyes flew wide. "There's been a breach—" The rest was drowned out by a sudden roar from the back of the throne room. To Lucian's disbelieving eyes, a horde of men in paramilitary garb—black body armor and masks and long barreled guns—streamed into the room, firing and trampling over the dragons closest to the door. Leonidas and Leksander and Lucian all shifted simultaneously. Leksander fell back to protect the king and queen, while Leonidas and Lucian surged forward. Tytus shifted and met Leonidas's charge talons-first. They grappled and fell to the ground. The throne room was in chaos—half had shifted to dragon form, the other half still in shock. But the black-armored men were mowing them down...

Something that shouldn't be possible.

Mere bullets couldn't stop a dragon. Lucian reached out with his fae senses as he surged forward through the crowd trying to reach the assault force…

They were all demons.

Holy fuck. Lucian's mind reeled—demon-possessed humans with military training. But conventional weapons *still* should have no effect against dragons. Yet Lucian watched in horror as one after another of the House of Smoke fell from the long-barreled guns aimed at them.

Lucian turned back to help Leonidas take down Tytus—cut off the head of the serpent, because Lucian was certain this was his doing—but to his horror, he found Tytus standing triumphant over Leonidas who was thrashing, eyes closed, on the floor. Tytus raised a fistful of talons to swipe down and cut off Leonidas's head. Lucian roared and surged forward, smacking into Tytus before he could end his brother's life. As he grappled with Tytus himself, confusion still rattled Lucian's brain —how could Tytus, a mere black dragon, take down Leonidas, a dragon with fae powers?

The answer came with a small stabbing pain in his side as Tytus punched something into him. A wave of sickness washed over Lucian, and his grip loosened on the black dragon. Something rushed Lucian's brain and made him dizzy. Tytus shoved him off, and Lucian couldn't even stay upright, tumbling back to the floor. There was a darkness crawling through his body. Tytus stood over him, holding a small pistol and laughing. The pistol had an unusually large barrel. When Lucian looked down at his side, he saw the dart sticking out. He plucked it and threw it away, but whatever it had injected into him had already found its target.

Poison. He didn't know what kind exactly, except that it was wrapping black tendrils around his heart and squeezing.

Chaos was still reigning behind Tytus, but it was clear that the black-armored military force he had commanded for the assault was winning.

Tytus held up the hand without the pistol. Through blurry vision, Lucian could tell that one of his talons was missing. "I had to make a small sacrifice for the darts, but seeing you writhe on the floor, Lucian Smoke, makes it all worthwhile." He raised his pistol and shot three more times behind Lucian. He heard the bodies fall, and he knew who they had to be—the king, the queen, and Leksander.

Tytus was killing all of them.

And once Lucian was dead... Tytus would go after Arabella and the baby.

That surged up a guttural roar inside Lucian that summoned every drop of fae magic he had in his blood. *"No!"* But it came out as a hoarse gasp. He closed his eyes to focus every healing spell he knew—every bit of magic he could conjure to fight this poison that was worming through his system.

Tytus's voice came closer. Lucian forced open his eyes. Tytus was down on one knee, peering at him and smirking. "I almost wish you would live long enough to see me take your mate."

Lucian wanted to rip out his throat, but he was still battling the poison, and it was seizing up his muscles, paralyzing him. All that could escape was a growl.

"Oh yes, I'll definitely enjoy her before I kill her. The dragonling of course will die. Then the Winter Court will give me dominion over the demons."

Lucian's breathing was becoming labored, but he focused hard on pushing the poison away from his brain—if he lost control there, he was done for. He made a tiny amount of headway, then a little more, and then the feeling started to come back into his arms. He feigned paralysis for a little longer, just a moment more, and then he would catch this bastard by surprise and cut off Tytus's head.

He kept talking. "You see, I've discovered their little loophole. For a people who cannot lie, the fae sure like their secrets. And they're surprisingly willing to negotiate when you have something over them. Like demons who are *created,* not *conjured.* But there's this little side effect. *Demons who are fully human.* And you know what doesn't work against humans? Magical wards." The smirk on his face was the smile of an idiot pleased with his one bit of treasure. The one piece of information that gave him power.

Lucian had never loathed Tytus more in his entire life.

"And now it's time for you to die, prince of the House of Smoke." Tytus raised a talon-filled hand.

Lucian couldn't wait for the poison to be gone. He lashed out with what strength he had, managing to bat away Tytus's talons and roll away from his deadly strike. A roar came from behind him, and suddenly Leonidas was on Tytus's back. The two took to wing and twirled through the throne room air, fighting and snarling and lashing. One of the humans took aim with his long-barreled dart gun and shot Leonidas. He growled his frustration, but the second dose of poison took him down hard. He dropped out of the air, and Tytus flapped away, retreating. Leksander somehow arose from the floor and was after him next, with Lucian close behind.

The tide was turning. His fellow dragons had finally realized what was happening and fashioned a defense against it. They had formed a battering ram out of their poisoned comrades, lifting the fallen dragon bodies and using them to smash the whole herd of human attackers into uselessness, guns knocked from their hands. Disarmed, they had no chance against the dragons. Leksander caught hold of Tytus's tail and whipped him back into Lucian's waiting talons. He grabbed hold of Tytus, but the weakness of the poison was still running through Lucian's system. He lost his grip, and Tytus twirled and took to wing again. He screeched some kind of sounding call, then soared to the top of the throne room, brushing his wings against the ceiling and then diving hard for the door.

He was making a run for it.

"I've got him!" Leksander shouted. "Go after your mate." His brother didn't wait for a reply, he just turned and flew over the hordes of demon-possessed humans to go after Tytus.

Lucian glanced back at Leonidas sprawled out

and writhing on the floor again. His mother and father were slumped in their thrones, not moving.

Fear seized his heart and battled with grief, but he had no time—he had to reach Arabella and the baby before Tytus's demon forces did.

Chapter Twelve

"I can't believe you're putting a sword up in a baby's room," Rachel complained for the third time. Her hands were parked on her hips, and her sigh was very audible.

All the gifts had been sorted and stacked in neat piles. One pile of gifts they would have to somehow regift or pack away because they were slightly disturbing—like the dragon eye carved out of glittering stone and mounted on a rock. Just creepy. One pile was things that were outright dangerous, like the sprig of green leaves and white flowers that smelled like raspberries. She didn't know much about babies, but leaving around magical herbs was probably not on the Smart Parenting list. And then there was the pile of things that were awesome, but she had no idea what to do with until the baby was older, like the Dragon Tales book that was written entirely in dragontongue. At least, she assumed it was dragontongue. They were symbols she couldn't read, but she assumed Lucian could read it to her when he was done with his official duties.

"I really miss him." Arabella sighed. Lucian Junior in her belly gave her a good poke of agreement. She rubbed that part to soothe him.

Rachel snapped her fingers in front of Arabella's face. "Pay attention! I'm complaining about weaponry in your nursery."

Arabella grinned. "It's not a sword, it's just a short blade. And it's supposed to be protective or something. It's not like the baby's going to climb the wall and grab it." Arabella had managed to find a couple of nails for the wall. The blade rested on them, balanced just right so it wouldn't fall. In truth, it wasn't very secure.

"But you're right—when Lucian gets back, I'll ask him to find a better way to secure the blade. In case we have an earthquake or some wall-shaking sex."

Rachel shook her head. "You two are still going at it, aren't you?"

Arabella's smile grew. "Every chance we get."

Rachel scowled. "Well, that'll have to come to an end after the baby's born. Everything I've read says that the sex just is *over* once there's a baby on the scene."

Arabella cocked an eyebrow. "Maybe for normal humans," she said with a smirk. "But we're talking dragon shifter mated sex, Rach. I really do recommend it." She waggled her eyebrows.

Rachel rolled her eyes. "Don't start on that again. I'm not saying Cinaed isn't hot—"

A crash came from outside the nursery. There was a moment of silence, then it sounded like a hundred feet stomping at once.

Rachel's eyes went wide. "What the fuck is that?"

Arabella shook her head fast and backed away from the door, which was closed. "I don't like this —" The door flew open. Two men in black with very large guns burst through. They whipped the barrels up to point at them.

A *thwick* sound pierced the air. Something smacked into Arabella's chest.

Rachel screamed, and Arabella staggered backward, one hand on her belly, the other reaching back to the wall. There was a dart sticking out of her chest! She held herself up by gripping the wall and managed to yank the dart out. The yelling and stomping and screaming men—big and hulking and dressed in black armor—flooded into the nursery. Darkness crowded her vision, and a sudden anger came over her. *They were after her baby.* She shoved away the darkness and reached above her to grab the angel blade off the wall. The men were holding back, watching them, waiting... then one rushed toward her, reaching for the blade. She evaded his grasp and stabbed for his neck. She missed, but the blade cut through his body armor like it was butter, sinking to the hilt in the man's chest. He screamed, and the unholy sound reverberated throughout the room. Arabella jerked away at the sight of a black, vaporous spirit writhing at the edges of the man's body. He slumped to the floor, and the black spirit-monster disappeared.

Everyone came to a halt.

Arabella braced against the wall and knelt down as best she could to snatch the angel blade back out of the man's chest.

She held it high as she crouched. "Stay back! All of you!"

Rachel struggled against the man-monster

holding her. Arabella could see the black vapor leaking at the edges of him as well.

"You fucking heard her—stay back!" Rachel screamed.

He wasn't paying attention to her. He just stared slack-jawed at the fallen man.

Rachel wriggled free and edged along the wall to Arabella's side. Then Rachel held out her fists as if she would punch anyone who dared come close. The dart was still lodged in her shoulder.

The blackness of whatever the dart had injected into Arabella still squirmed around inside her. The baby kicked and fought against it, and that set off a huge cramp that made Arabella gasp and double over. She tried to keep the angel blade up, but she was barely staying off the floor. Rachel grabbed the blade and held it high, brandishing it at the men.

They stepped backed with freaked-out looks on their faces, glancing at one another.

"You okay?" Rachel asked in a hoarse whisper, one hand on Arabella's shoulder to keep her upright.

The cramp passed as Arabella felt glowing white magic rally and swirl a protective blanket around her baby, warding off the black tendrils, whatever they were.

"Yeah," she gasped. "I'm okay." She said it as much for the men's benefit as for Rachel's. The fact that she and Rachel were fighting back and hadn't been taken out by their darts seemed to have completely thrown them.

Arabella struggled up to standing.

Only then could she see between the men and out through the doorway. Cinaed was on the ground, writhing back and forth in some kind of torment.

It suddenly clicked in Arabella's brain. "Poison."

Rachel dashed a look to her. "What?"

Arabella plucked the dart barrel from Rachel's shoulder and threw it back at the men in black armor. They cringed away.

"Fucking dragon poison." She ran a quick look over Rachel, who didn't seem to be in any discomfort. "Must not work on humans." But Rachel sent a worried look to Arabella's belly. "Baby's okay," Arabella said quietly. "I think that angel blessing was worth something after all."

Rachel nodded and held the blade out, but then she caught sight of Cinaed, and her face twisted with anger and pure hatred. She brandished the angel blade again. "You motherfuckers! Which one of you fuckers wants to die next!"

But Arabella could hear the hiked-up fear in her voice, and she knew just what Rachel was thinking —if these assholes could get past Cinaed, then what was happening with the rest of the House? If they had reached *the nursery*—did that mean Lucian was already dead? Arabella shoved those thoughts aside. She had to focus on staying alive and protecting her baby—everything else came last.

The men in black were muttering amongst themselves, eyeing the two women, but not actually making a move. Keeping their distance.

Another one came tromping down the hall. He tapped one of the men inside the nursery on the shoulder. He leaned back, and the first one whispered something in his ear.

Then that one turned to Rachel and Arabella. "You two. You're coming with us."

"Just try and take us, asshole!" Rachel said, holding out the blade. The one who seemed to be in charge gave a short nod to the guy standing in front of him, who was still training his long dart gun on them. He slung the gun around to his back and advanced slowly.

"You want to end up like your buddy on the floor?" Rachel screeched, brandishing the angel weapon, but with a lot of panic in her voice.

The man watched her warily, edging closer, hands out—then he made his move. He lurched forward and grabbed hold of her, his beefy arms going around to capture Rachel's. She struggled and then managed to twist the knife and shove it up into his body armor. As far as Arabella could see, it sunk in deep. The man went down, but he took Rachel with him. The rest suddenly surged forward, with a half dozen more coming in through the door, all coordinated in some kind of synchronous attack. They swarmed over Arabella. A dozen hands were on her, gripping her arms and legs and hoisting her up into the air, belly to the ceiling. She wanted to struggle, but there was no way she could escape them.

"Rachel!" she screamed.

"Let go of me, you asshole!" There was a lot of grunting, and Rachel's voice shouting and cursing... and then a sudden silence.

Arabella twisted her head back as they carried her out of the nursery, but she couldn't see anything over the sea of black bodies that had piled on Rachel.

"No, no, no," she whispered. Tears pooled at the corners of her eyes, but there was nothing she could do. She squeezed her eyes shut and gritted her teeth as the men carried her out of Lucian's lair.

Chapter Thirteen

He was too late.

As Lucian stumbled into his lair, he didn't even have to reach the nursery or call out for Arabella to know she was already gone. The front door had been torn off its hinges. A trample of boot marks scuffed the entryway. His heart was frozen in his chest as he lumbered around the corner to the great room, following the moaning sound.

It was Cinaed on the floor, clenched up and frozen. More destruction lay a path toward the nursery where the door stood open. The ancient cradle passed down through generations of his family was smashed. He hesitated only briefly then trudged on wooden legs toward the nursery room itself. He fully expected to find Arabella's body torn to shreds. He staggered up to the doorway and gripped the edge of it, bracing himself.

But the room was empty.

Well, not entirely empty.

Two of Tytus's demon-thugs lay sprawled on the floor. One had the angel blade sticking out of his vest. They were moaning and weakened, but they weren't dead—Lucian's fae senses told him the demons who had possessed them were gone. He gave a silent, heartbreaking thanks to Erelah for giving Arabella a fighting chance. It looked like she had gotten one of the attackers, but after the second one, they must've overwhelmed her.

They've taken her. As that thought beat past the panic and the grief to sink into his brain, he realized that she must still be alive. Or at least, there was a strong possibility of it.

His chest loosened enough so he could breathe again. She had fought them, but for some reason, they hadn't killed her. Instead, they had taken her—and probably Rachel too, given that Arabella's friend was missing from the lair as well. Now that his worst fears hadn't yet come true, his brain started functioning again. He turned and stumbled back to Cinaed, who was still writhing on the ground, suffering from the poison. How many dragons had already died from this very thing? Lucian couldn't think about that right now. His only priority was to find Arabella and the baby, and for that, he needed Cinaed.

He hurried to kneel by his best friend's side. The poison had locked him up so badly, he couldn't speak. Lucian knew exactly how that felt. He pressed his hands to Cinaed's face and chest and focused his healing fae magic to reach inside to the demon-sourced poison. It was curling around Cinaed's body and killing him. A long moment later, Cinaed gasped in a breath as his lungs opened up again.

His first gasping words were, "They took her."

"I know," Lucian ground out. "Breathe for a moment, my friend. Let me heal you. I'll need your strength to help go after them." Then Lucian closed his eyes and focused again on banishing the curling black sickness that was still worming through his best friend's body. Lucian didn't open his eyes again until most of it was gone. In the process, he recognized there were still traces weakening his own body. He didn't have time to worry about that—he was functional enough.

"Was Tytus here?" Lucian asked as he gave a hand to Cinaed and helped him up from the floor. His friend almost toppled over but managed to stay upright, blinking and shaking his head.

"Tytus?" Cinaed coughed out. "This is his doing? No, he wasn't here. At least, I didn't see him." He paused to pull in another deep breath, then gestured for Lucian to follow him toward the front door. "They were human, mercenaries, with some kind of poison darts. They tried to kill the girls, but my Rachel fought them. Arabella too."

"I surmised as much. Do you know where they went?"

Cinaed was still shaking his head free of the poison's effects. "No, but I think the poison did not work on Rachel and Arabella. There was some kind of hushed discussion, but I couldn't hear it. The attackers were communicating with someone else, remotely."

Lucian narrowed his eyes. "If the poison didn't work… they must be bringing them to Tytus. Even with the protections that Arabella has, she has no defense against dragon talons."

Cinaed nodded, then his eyes went wide with realization. "Tytus has infiltrated the rest of the keep?"

"Yes. Many are down. My brothers and I managed to fight back, and Tytus fled like the coward he is." Anger clouded his brain, and he forced it away—he had to remain levelheaded. "Where would Tytus go?"

"The question, my lord, is how did the mercenaries breach the keep?"

"What does that matter now?" Lucian growled. "They've already broken through—"

"It matters because they will likely leave the same way."

Lucian pounded a fist into his forehead. "Of course, you're right."

How could he not have thought of that? His mind was compromised by pain and grief and fear and worry. He struggled to push all that aside.

"My lord, they may have had an armory of poison darts with them, but they *were* human."

"No, they were demons."

Cinaed scowled at that. "Nonetheless, they did not shift and fly in."

"The garage." Lucian finally caught his meaning.

"Just so."

The two of them made a dash for the elevators of

Lucian's private entrance down to the garage. There was no evidence of the mercenaries' passing, but they may have been able to simply walk in—the keep was proofed against immortal creatures not humans who somehow could see past the glamour that hid it from human eyes. Tytus's troops likely simply walked in.

Lucian growled in frustration, then patted his pockets, searching for a phone to call his brothers, but he had lost his in the fight. Cinaed pulled one from his pocket instead.

Lucian tapped in the number and prayed to all that was magic that Leksander had already managed to capture Tytus and kill the bastard.

After two rings it picked up. "Cinaed, is the princess secure?" Leksander asked.

"It's me," Lucian said. "Arabella is gone. Did you stop Tytus from escaping?"

His brother swore brightly in dragontongue. "No. There were more hordes coming in through the royal gate, and he slipped away outside. Many dragons were down, and I was still suffering from the poison…" A horrible weariness came over the line in Leksander's voice.

"Leonidas?" Lucian asked, his heart clenched.

"Alive. I've been healing him. He was healing

the others and was almost gone…" There was more, but Leksander wasn't speaking it.

Lucian's heart stuttered. "The king and queen." He couldn't bear to make it a question. They were already on in years…

"The queen lives." There was heartbreak that reached through the line and threatened to choke Lucian.

The elevator down to the garage came to a stop, and Lucian and Cinaed stumbled out into the glare of the underground parking lot lights. Black skid-marks crisscrossed the concrete, telling the tale of the assault vehicles that had been here not long ago. Those black lines tore like a laser through Lucian's grief and focused his mind.

"The demons have taken Arabella," he said. "I'm sure they mean to bring her to Tytus so he can finish the job with his talons."

"You go after them," Leksander said, a rumbling growl in his voice. "Leonidas and I will gather those who are still standing and follow."

"The demons can't have gotten far," Lucian said, partly to reassure himself, but partly because it had to be true.

"Fly, my brother," Leksander said. "Avenge our father. I'll see what other forces I can muster."

Lucian hung up the phone. "Let's go," he said to Cinaed.

His best friend eyed the single black sedan left in the underground parking lot. "Flying is faster," he said.

They shifted and headed out of the garage into the bright afternoon sun.

Chapter Fourteen

THE DEMONS FINALLY PUT ARABELLA DOWN.

Then they shoved her into one of several Humvees, and the entire group took off like they thought Lucian and a horde of angry dragons would be after them in a heartbeat. At least, Arabella hoped that would be true. The demon-men had knocked out Rachel, but they'd also brought her along. Her best friend lay limp on the seat next to her, her head lolled to the side and resting on Arabella's shoulder. The angel blade was gone, left behind at Lucian's lair during the fight.

Rachel and Arabella were hemmed in on either side by hulking mercenaries in black body armor. They were silent and stoic, but Arabella could see the demons inside them, black essences of anger and hatred. There were three more in the front seat of the Humvee, the driver and two others. They were all demon-infected. That first night that Lucian saved her from a half-demon, half-human in the alleyway outside her office, she hadn't known anything about the immortal world. The guy who attacked her just seemed like one more asshole in a world filled with assholes, only Arabella had the bad luck of ending up in a dark alley alone with one. Now she could literally *see* the evil in these men. Her life seemed irrevocably different now… but once again, it seemed perilously close to ending in the next few minutes. Lucian had rescued her before—she had to have faith he would do it again.

She hugged the baby in her belly with one hand and braced Rachel against the jostling of the Humvee with the other. Then Arabella prayed desperately to whatever gods and guardian angels might be out there that all three of them would make it through this.

The demons first attempt at killing her had failed… so they had to be taking her somewhere they could try again. As the Humvee wound through the curvy mountain roads that led up to the keep, she couldn't help but wonder how everything had gone so wrong so fast. How her love could be

True, how she could have rescued Lucian from the mire of his doubts and fears, how she could've survived the sealing and the pregnancy and made it to the cusp of bringing her precious baby boy into the world… only to have it all unravel.

All because *someone* wanted her dead. Or more specifically, her baby.

She was convinced Zephan was behind it, in spite of Lucian's assurances that it was impossible. Whoever these men were—these demon-infected humans that she could now see because she was filled with her own dragon magic—they were just minions for someone else.

And wherever they were going, that someone else was going to kill her baby.

The baby rolled over in response to all the crazy anxiety that was rocketing through her body. As he did, that white burning force of the blessing that she felt protecting him in the womb turned with him. The inky blackness of the poison was still in her system—she could feel it weakening her arms and gripping her stomach tight. And as the Humvee bumped along the road and jostled her, and one minute stretched into another, it felt like that shield was weakening.

When they took a tight turn that rocked her

hard, something turned inside her, and suddenly, a tightness gripped her belly as if in a giant vise.

"Oh!" she gasped, hunching over in her seat and holding tighter onto her belly. She could feel her son thrashing inside her. "No, baby no, it's okay," she whispered. She rubbed the spots where he was poking, but it didn't help. The tightening at the base of her belly just grew and rolled like a wave across her stomach ending in a pulling-apart feeling that seemed like it was ripping her in two. *"Ahhh!"* It was half gasp, half scream.

The thug in the seat next to her dashed a look at her, frowning.

But she couldn't even pay attention to that—the wave was starting again at the bottom of her belly, only twice as tight, twice as hard, and three times as painful.

This time, she let out a moan that was mostly scream.

Rachel startled awake next to her. The bruise was just starting to take on her face, and Arabella hated to see it, but she couldn't think about anything through the haze of pain cycling through her body, clenching and unclenching in waves.

"What—" Rachel looked around. *"What the fuck."* Then she looked back to Arabella. "Ari, honey, are you okay?" she gasped out, one hand going to Ari's back to rub it and the other slipping on top of Ari's clenched fist on her leg.

"*Rachel,*" Arabella eeked out, but she couldn't say anymore through the pain. She wanted to say she was sorry for getting her best friend involved in all this. Especially when it seemed like they were on a one-way trip to their deaths. But all she could think about was the baby. "The baby's coming," she managed.

The mercenary on the other side of Rachel jerked to attention. He rapped on the plexiglass that separated them from the front. "We've got a situation back here."

The man in the front seat looked her over and seemed uncertain.

Arabella rocked back and forth because it seemed to ease the pain a little.

Rachel rubbed Arabella's back harder. "Okay, honey, just breathe through it." She leaned over to peer into Arabella's eyes. "You are *not* having that baby in this Humvee, you understand me? You need to hold on."

Arabella nodded. If they were to have any chance to escape, she couldn't be in labor during it. She had to be able to *run.* But then the next wave hit, and she was moaning and trying to bite back the scream, but it was no use. Her wailing seemed to thoroughly freak out the mercenaries who were on either side of them.

Now the second one was pounding on the front. "You need to park this thing!"

Some kind of argument ensued between the front and the back, grunts and yelling, but all Arabella could hear was her own screaming in her ears, and the white-hot pain that felt like it was slicing her open. She got through the next round, but all the air had been sucked out of her. She panted and tried to pull in a breath, gripping Rachel's hand so hard she was afraid she might hurt it. A cold sweat broke out all over Arabella's body.

"Not…" she panted. "Not going to make it."

"The hell you're not!" Rachel joined in with the chorus of yelling, and just as the next wave started to hit and pull Arabella into a haze of pain and screaming, the car swerved to the side of the road and slipped under a canopy of trees. It continued up a steep incline, then they reached a level spot, and the Humvee jerked to a stop.

Arabella creaked her eyes open—they were surrounded by trees overhead and on every side. *How would Lucian find them now?* Because she was convinced he was still alive, and if there was one thing she knew about Lucian Smoke, it was that as long as blood was still pumping through his veins, he would come after her.

There was a tiny sliver of blue sky out the front window of the Humvee, past the other cars, and down the length of the broken pavement road that seemed to lift up into the heavens. Arabella focused on that small patch of sky and willed Lucian to see them through it. Her vision telescoped down through the pain in her belly to that singular hope.

Rachel was jabbering at her and petting her arm and brushing the hair back from her sweaty, sweaty face. Arabella focused on breathing through the pain as the next wave grappled with her. She needed to survive. This baby needed to survive. Her only job was to make sure that happened. She closed her eyes and focused on sending soothing waves to the baby, who was now churning and pushing and poking like he never had before. *It's okay, baby. We're going to make it through this.* She gave all of her love to him, every ounce that she had for Lucian, every bit that had been growing steadily inside her for this tiny little being who depended completely on her. *We can do this,* she told him.

The wave passed, and then the next one, and

the next after that… she lost count after a while. The car had fallen silent under her moaning and keening. When she was worn from it, bone weary, and needed the reassurance of that blue patch of sky one more time, she creaked open her eyes, wiped the sweat from the corners, and focused on it.

Her heart stuttered when a winging black shape came into focus, flying straight down that little blue patch.

She would've smiled if she had any energy for it.

"Oh my God," Rachel said, but it wasn't with the relief Arabella expected.

Arabella blinked and blinked again… and then focused on the thin black wings that were pumping their way across the blue sky.

Black wings.

Lucian was a golden dragon.

Arabella's heart stuttered with the remembered fear of what that black shape meant—*Tytus.*

And then a flush of heat washed through her that was stronger than any magical fire she had ever felt. The baby jumped and poked, and the fire flared like it might all of a sudden consume her.

The scream she let out this time emptied her out, body and soul.

Chapter Fifteen

LUCIAN USED EVERY SENSE HE HAD TO SCAN THE rolling mountains beneath him.

They can't have gone this far. Cinaed sent the thought to him as he soared next to Lucian, his blue scales glistening in the hot afternoon sun.

Maybe they didn't stick to the road, Lucian thought in return. He broadened his scans to the sides of the mountains around the winding pavement below them. *Those demon-infected humans were paramilitary. They could've brought an all-terrain vehicle for all we know.*

What if they pulled off early on? Cinaed's thought was ringed with worry.

Lucian knew his prime concern was finding Arabella and the baby, but he was also just as certain his best friend was worried about his new ladylove, Rachel.

I can't believe we missed them. Lucian banked away from Cinaed and made a circle doubling back and scanning the area, as well as climbing into the air to get a wider reach.

How far can you sense, my lord? Cinaed asked.

Not far enough. A growl rumbled in Lucian's chest.

We made haste in leaving the keep, Cinaed thought. *It's possible we missed them.*

Fuck. They were nearly to the edge of the mountain range that dipped down into Seattle. Cinaed was right. Even if Tytus's demon army was going a hundred miles an hour in whatever vehicle they had, they couldn't have come this far already. Lucian turned back.

I'll go low and scan for any roads that split off from the main one, Cinaed thought.

I'll go high and reach as far as I can. Lucian didn't need to tell his best friend to hurry. The creeping sense that they were already too late was itching up Lucian's golden scales, just as his runes were writhing all over his body, from the tip of his snout, back along his spine, to the end of his tail. As he and Cinaed doubled back, Lucian's heart sank deeper into a black dread at what they would find when they reached Arabella.

If they found her at all.

Visions of his previous mate drenched in blood flashed up in his mind. He shoved that away. The only blood he would see today would be Tytus's dripping from his talons. But only if Lucian could reach him before he caught up to Arabella. And Tytus had the distinct advantage of knowing where his demons actually were.

Lucian stopped the curses running through his head and focused solely on spreading his fae senses out to the forest below him. The trees were thick and impenetrable to any kind of visual scanning. He should be able to sense the demons, but Tytus's words were haunting him. *They are fully human.* That explained why Lucian had such difficulty finding the demons in Seattle and how they waltzed through the wards of the keep. His mind was still wrapping around how that was possible and how this horde came to be, but he would sort that out later. Right now, he couldn't rely on his fae senses to detect the demon inside the men, at least, not at a distance. But these woods should be unoccupied—

any humans at all would be a telltale sign, and Lucian would recognize his own mate's scent easiest of all. So that's what he focused on—imagining Arabella and his son, who was almost ready to leave her womb and enter the world and fulfill everything that Lucian lived for. He held them tight in his mind and cast his senses out as far as they would go. He held just as hard to the hope that he would find them before it was too late.

My lord! Cinaed's thoughts jabbed into his own.

Do you have them? Lucian focused intently on the blue dragon flying below him.

Cinaed banked right then slammed into a rough landing on the ground. *No, but I have a call.* He shifted human and fished a phone out of his pocket. It was possible to carry a phone while in dragon form if one took care when shifting to tuck it inside the bony flaps on the back of one's wings. Lucian had no time for such things in the fight in the throne room.

He soared down. His talons bit into the gravel on the side of the road, bringing him to a fast and hard stop next to Cinaed. Lucian's wings folded as he shifted human again.

"Yes," Cinaed was saying quickly. "We're about

ten miles out. No, we'll be right there." He swiped off the phone and said to Lucian, "We have help. Leksander and Erelah have summoned her angel faction leader, Markos. He says he knows where the demons are."

"What are they waiting for?" Lucian itched to shift again. "Let's go!"

Cinaed scowled. "The angel says he cannot interfere directly—he can only lead us there. And he'll only speak to you, Lucian."

"Fucking angels," Lucian spat. "Where are they?"

"At the keep." Cinaed didn't waste time with any more words—he just leaped into the air and shifted into his dragon form.

Lucian followed, and with his fae magic boosting him, he quickly moved ahead of Cinaed. In less than half a minute, he was nearing the keep. The angel stood on the rooftop, glowing with power. Erelah was at his side, angel blade in hand— he had never been more glad to see her. Lucian would be happy to slay every demon involved in kidnapping Arabella, but that would take time—he could slaughter them outright, but Erelah could separate the demon from the man, and in spite of everything, Lucian had no taste for killing humans, if he could avoid it. He was a protector of humanity, not a killer. Not like Tytus. Erelah would make much quicker work of the demons with her blade, leaving the humans a chance at surviving.

Standing on the rooftop beside the angel and angeling were Leksander and Leonidas and a dozen dragons from the House. Lucian didn't want to think about whether that was all they had left. Leksander's face was grave, but Leonidas looked outright sick—a gray pallor had taken hold of his face. His look of determination seemed to be all that kept him standing.

Lucian quickly landed on the roof and demanded of the angel, "Where is she?"

"Your human mate is in grave danger," he said, his voice booming.

Lucian's heart squeezed so hard, he felt it might burst. "I fucking *know* that, Angel!" He jabbed a quickly-formed talon in the asshole's face. *"Where is she?"*

"I cannot say," he said, utterly unconcerned about the threat Lucian was posing with his body and his voice. "And I can only direct you to the demons. I cannot assist. Do you understand?"

"Yes, yes. *Talk!*" Lucian was ready to rip it out of the angel's mouth.

Cinaed came to a skittering halt on the rooftop behind him, just catching up.

"Follow me." The angel unfurled his broad, white wings as he lifted magically from the roof. A warrior glint shone in Erelah's eyes as she leaped into the air as well, blade in hand, her wings majestically unfolding. Lucian leaped after them with Cinaed on his tail. Leonidas, Leksander, and the other dragons of the House quickly shifted and followed. Lucian could feel the sickness of the poison still circulating through his body, and Leonidas looked even worse—his flying was neither straight nor steady. The angel climbed and climbed into the air and flew far too slowly for Lucian's taste. He was ready to screech at the oversized immortal if he didn't pick up the pace, but as it turned out, they didn't have far to go.

Markos halted suddenly, mid-air.

The dragons had to circle back to where he had stopped.

"This is as close as I can get." He pointed a single finger down toward the earth. "There."

Lucian saw nothing with his eyes—until the

movement of a thin black figure skimming the tree-tops caught his attention. There was no question in his mind who it was. *Tytus.*

Lucian immediately dove after him, shoving a thought toward Cinaed as he went. *Take Erelah and find the demons—and Arabella.*

I will protect her with my life, Cinaed responded. Then he spoke out loud, his dragon form using dragontongue, a language ancient and screeching, but it was one the angeling could understand. Erelah's angel-warrior cry sounded in response, and she took off like a shot—far faster than Cinaed or even Lucian could manage. Cinaed dove after her, toward the canopy, running ahead of Lucian and the beeline he was making for the dark silhouette that was skimming the treetops.

We have your back, my brother, came the thought from Leksander behind him. And Lucian had no doubt that his brothers and the other dragons were out for Tytus's blood, but there was no one who was going to reach the black dragon before him.

As Lucian plummeted through the air, Tytus whipped a quick look up into the air. Either he heard Cinaed's cry or he just sensed Lucian's murderous intent, but his black eyes locked with

Lucian's for just a split second… then Tytus looked forward and flew even faster.

He wasn't breaking or turning or sweeping away—or even diving below the canopy to hide.

That could only mean one thing.

Tytus was racing to reach Arabella *first.*

Chapter Sixteen

"OH MY GOD, OH MY GOD, OH MY GOD," RACHEL screeched.

The mantra wasn't helping Arabella.

Then again, nothing really could at this point. The contraction had subsided, but she was burning up, and the baby was threatening to claw his way out of her womb. Tears were running down her face with the pain, and she was gripping the seat in front of her in the Humvee, panting and trying to simply hold on until the next wave of pain hit.

The demon thugs were arguing back and forth, front seat to back. All their voices were jittering and ricocheting around in her brain—all sound and no meaning.

"Oh my God, Arabella." The panic in Rachel's

voice was the only thing that got through to her. Her hands on Arabella's arms and face felt ice cold next to the raging heat that was her flesh. "Oh my God, you're burning up."

"Too hot," Arabella agreed, but it was a whisper. She could hardly form words through the thick haze of pain and the suffering, choking feeling of her lungs filling with fire.

Suddenly, something was jostling her… and it wasn't her baby doing somersaults inside her, trying to escape the heat that was threatening to burn them both into ash. More hands were on her, on the other side from Rachel—big, rough hands, hauling her sideways.

"What are you *doing?*" Rachel demanded. "Can't you see she's having a baby!"

"Out of the car!" a man said with a gruff voice. Then he followed it up with a rough tug on her arm that slid her halfway across the Humvee's slick leather seating.

The pain of the labor and the heat of the fire left her limp. She had no power to resist at all. But it also made her dead weight and awkward. The thug finally climbed out of the car then reached back for her, but it was still hard for him to drag her out of the car.

But he managed it.

Arabella's legs couldn't hold her—she fell, her knees digging into the gravel through her jeans. She threw her hands out, catching herself before she landed belly-first on the ground.

"Oh my God, you fucking assholes!" Rachel must've clambered out of the car after her. Her best friend crashed down next to her, an arm protectively gripping Arabella's shoulders while she was on hands and knees in the dirt.

Then the tightening began again.

The pain was somehow worse than the fire that was consuming her from the inside out. It started even lower in her belly now, squeezing and pulling at the same time, then climbing up her back, making it arch with the wrenching pain. Her moan quickly climbed up into a scream again as it reached the peak.

Rachel's hands were smoothing her cheeks and her forehead and pulling her sopping wet hair off her face, but none of it did anything but give Arabella a tiny sliver of coolness. She focused on that and the love behind the hands. *Hold on, baby,* she said to her unborn son. *Daddy's coming. I know he is. Just hold on.*

The peak of the contraction passed, and the

pain started to wind down, but the fire was still ramping up. Arabella was panting, breathing in the hot, dusty, roadside air—even that was cooler than the fire inside her. Boots scraped the ground next to her, and suddenly, someone yanked Rachel away from her side. Screams and protests and curses were met with another bone-smacking sound that made Arabella's whole body jerk.

"Don't hurt her," she panted, but it was just a whisper. And she knew the demon-men didn't care anyway.

Their hands were on her, lifting her up from the ground. Her toes dragged in the gravel as they carried her away from the cars and toward the forest. It was only a dozen feet away, and it beckoned, dark and cool. The fire in Arabella's brain longed for it. But a part of her knew that this was a bad, bad thing. If they could hide her, buying time until that black dragon in the sky could reach her, Arabella wouldn't survive two seconds beyond that.

And neither would her baby.

Somewhere from the depths of her being, she gathered up the strength to fight—she had to slow them down, do anything she could to stop them.

She dug her feet into the dirt. She squirmed in the hold of their clumsy hands. Her body was so slick with sweat, she was like a greased eel. She wormed one arm free, then redoubled her efforts with the other one. One man swore and grabbed at her harder. Another dug fingers even deeper into her arm. Just as they got a grip on her again, the air cracked all around them.

A fiery blur of white fell from heaven and landed with a ground-shaking thud in front of them. Arabella's vision was blurred with pain and heat. Sweat was dripping into her eyes and making her squint. It took her a second, but when she blinked them clear, could see who it was...

Erelah.

With a raised blade and a look of righteous fury and power, the angeling's scream shook the air and made the arms holding Arabella tremble. Erelah surged forward and sank her blade into the demon on her left. He jerked away from Arabella and fell to the ground. In a blur, Erelah swiped the blade in an arc, up then down, plunging into the demon to her right. His body dragged Arabella down, its grip still hard even as the man's head lolled back... but Erelah caught her in an angelic hug that vibrated with power and set her free.

"I have you, princess of the House of Smoke!" Erelah cried triumphantly.

Arabella slumped in her arms. "Too hot," she gasped.

Erelah's eyes went wide, staring at her in horror and confusion.

Rachel appeared at Arabella's side, grabbing hold of her other arm. "She's burning up!" she yelled. "You have to help her!"

Erelah released her, and Rachel struggled to hold her up.

"I don't... I know not how..." Erelah shrank a little and looked terribly uncertain. Then her gaze was caught by the other demon thugs who were fleeing. "Her death is upon you!" she shouted, raising her blade and going after them. Arabella heard their screams as the angeling caught them, but that didn't matter. None of that would save her and the baby.

Rachel couldn't hold her up when her legs buckled. Arabella sank to the ground as another wave of pain started deep in her belly. Rachel cradled her in her arms and started petting her again with cool hands.

Arabella leaned into them and managed to gasp out the words that needed to be said. "The baby. You have to save the baby, Rach."

"No! I'm saving *you!*" But there was terror in her

eyes. And they both knew there was nothing she could do.

Then a flap of wings beat the air, and Arabella felt it wash over her. Terror clawed at her heart as she blinked away the sweat and the sun. *Was Tytus here already?* But there was a blue dragon landing instead, sending up a puff of dirt next to Rachel and transforming into a man.

Cinaed dropped to his knees, one arm around Rachel and the other on Arabella's belly. "My lady!" he cried. "The baby? Are you well?"

"She's burning up!" Rachel sobbed. "Cinaed, do something!"

He leaned back and waved his hands, conjuring a tub filled with ice water next to her. Then he scooped up Arabella, wrenching her away from Rachel's grasp, and hurried her into the water. It was a welcome splash of coolness, but the fire had been raging too long and too deep. Steam rose off Arabella's body and drenched the air above them.

"No, no, no!" Rachel was crying, tears running down her face.

Cinaed knelt by the edge of the tub, splashing water over her belly. "Hold fast, my lady! The prince is coming."

Lucian. He's alive. But the pain was climbing up

her back again, and Arabella couldn't speak. Moaning turned to keening and then to screaming. She curled up over her belly with the strength of it, rocking and splashing the water in the tub.

Cinaed's face held panic. Rachel was sobbing. Erelah arrived at the side of the tub looking thoroughly terrified at the sight of Arabella thrashing in the water.

The pain peaked and subsided again. Arabella sagged back in the tub. Only Cinaed's quick hand kept her head from going under. Arabella weakly pawed the air and the side of the tub, searching for Erelah's hand. When she found it, she grabbed hold of it with all the strength she had left, which was practically nothing, and urged the angeling closer.

Erelah bent down, her eyes wide, to hear Arabella's whispered plea. "Use your blade," she gasped. "Take the baby."

Erelah leaned back, eyes lit with horror. "I cannot... *no!*"

"Please. Save my baby." But that was all she could say, the last of her strength sapping out of her. Darkness started to crowd in on her vision. Arabella closed her eyes and leaned back to get as much of her body in the water as possible. She focused in on the baby deep inside. Past the raging fire. Past the waves of pain that were wracking her. Down to the baby who was churning and churning inside her, fighting for his life. *Daddy's coming*, she thought. *Just hold on. Just hold on…*

She believed it with all her heart—Lucian *would* come for her.

But she didn't know if it would be soon enough.

Chapter Seventeen

Erelah's warrior-angel cry reached Lucian's ears just as he closed in on Tytus from above.

Lucian was diving snout first, wings swept back so he could rocket down, but just as he reached Tytus's leathery black wings, the bastard barrel rolled—and clutched in his talons was a gun. Three short pops blew darts into Lucian's chest just as he smacked into Tytus, now flying upside down. The impact knocked them both out of the sky and into the canopy below. As they crashed and tumbled through the leaves, Lucian felt the triple dose of poison leech through his system, carried even faster by his rapid-beating heart, hyped on adrenaline and anger and fear. He smacked into the ground with such force that he bounced, and that was the only thing that allowed him to get his legs under him before he landed again. Tytus was a short ways off, crashing and rolling through the underbrush. Lucian staggered after him, marshaling all of his fae magic to combat the poison—now that he knew what it was, it was easier to fight, but it still felt like a lead weight dragging behind him. Tytus glanced back and saw Lucian slicing small trees out of his way with his talons and stumbling after, so he leaped into the air, whirled on black wings, and pivoted to rake Lucian with a blast of dragonfire. Lucian drew his wings over his face, but the fire still scorched him as he lifted off the ground. With no room to maneuver in the dense spacing of trees, Lucian tipped sideways and drove between the narrow columns toward Tytus, reaching him before Tytus could get off another fireball. Lucian sank his talons into the black scales of his chest, and even with Lucian's strength sapped by the poison, he was able to throw Tytus to the ground.

The trees above cracked and snapped as the other dragons—Leksander and Leonidas and the remaining dragons of his House—dove into the forest.

But Tytus was his to kill.

Lucian had him pinned to the forest floor, his

talons sunk deep into Tytus's chest. Blood surged out of his gaping and panting mouth. "You are weak," he gurgled. "My demons will kill her before you can—" Lucian cut off his vile words with a squeeze that made Tytus scream. Then Lucian wrenched one blood-covered set of talons out of Tytus's chest and swiped it across his neck, severing his head and sending it rolling into the ferns.

Lucian's breath heaved, the poison making him weaker by the second, and he had to struggle to pull his other hand from Tytus's now dead body. Lucian stood over the black dragon, wavering and dizzy, as Leonidas and Leksander both dropped through the last branches to the ground by Lucian's side.

He turned to them, and Leonidas reached forward to steady him, his talons gently gripping Lucian's shoulder to keep him upright. Runes rustled down Leonidas's arm, and Lucian could feel the magic flooding into him, the healing spell chasing after the dark tendrils of poison.

Leonidas shifted human and plucked the three darts from Lucian's chest, throwing them to the ground by Tytus's body. Lucian returned to human form as well.

"My brother," he gasped, his chest a tight

squeeze from the poison. "You don't have the energy to save me."

"Shut up," Leonidas said. He kept pumping healing energy into Lucian.

Leksander joined them on the other side, in human form as well, and did the same. Between his two brothers and their powerful magic, the poison began to quickly recede.

Lucian shook his head and shoved their hands away. "Arabella," he wheezed, his lungs still tight. Then he leaped into the air and fought his way through the branches to lift above the forest canopy. He reached out with his weakened fae senses—they couldn't go far, but less than a mile away, he sensed Arabella.

The strong, vibrant scent of her was weak... and fading. And the baby—

He pumped his wings and gave everything he had to speed across the canopy toward her.

We are with you, my brother, he heard in his mind. It was Leksander, crashing up through the canopy close behind him.

I sense the baby... Leonidas's thoughts were in a panic. *Lucian, hurry.*

Emotion surged up to choke Lucian, but he focused in like a laser on Arabella's scent. There was nothing but her now—her and the baby—and in a handful of seconds that seemed to stretch forever, he finally saw her through a small opening the tree line. She was lying in a tub of water between the road and the forest. He rocketed down in dragon form and landed, shifting to human as soon as his feet touched the ground. He hit it running and was by her side in an instant.

Erelah moved to make room for him. Lucian dropped to his knees next to the tub. Cinaed was holding her just barely above the water. Rachel huddled by the side, crying. Lucian could feel the heat coming off Arabella even before he touched her. Her eyes were closed, and she was mumbling something, delirious. Her skin was like fire when he touched her cheek and slipped his other hand to her belly where his son was writhing in torment. His runes rushed to his hands, and he began flooding her with the healing magic she needed.

He just didn't know if it would be enough.

His touch seemed to rouse her—her eyes popped open, and those beautiful green jewels stared up at him. She blinked, rapidly, and her eyes seem to be looking past him into some infinite distance.

"I'm here, my love," he whispered. He leaned

forward, dipping his head down and brushing his cheek against hers. "I'm here," he whispered in her ear.

She responded to that, turning her face to press against his. "The baby," she gasped. "Save our baby, Lucian."

He drew back, tears threatening his eyes. "I'm saving you *both.*"

Lucian heard his brothers land behind him, felt the beat of their wings folding as they shifted back to human. A fraction of a moment later, they arrived at his side, both plunging their hands into the icy water Cinaed had conjured to keep Arabella cool and finding a place on Arabella's hands or arms or legs in which to infuse her with their magic. Even weakened by poison—between the three of them, they were saturated with it—Lucian could feel the power of the three of them joining to carry her through.

He still didn't know if it would be enough.

Then Arabella cried out and lurched up out of the water, curling over her belly and keening a low moan that grew and grew in volume until she was screaming. Lucian fought to bring her back into the water, but she was curled up tight.

"My love," he said, a cry in his voice, "breathe

through it. You have to stay in the water. The heat..." Then he couldn't talk anymore, not over her cries of pain.

They were slicing through him like razor-sharp talons.

Rachel reached out both hands to Arabella's shoulders and gently urged Arabella to lay back in the water. "Ari, honey, you've got to stay in the water. Please stay in the water."

Leonidas's face was still ashen, but he leaned forward until he was close to Arabella's ear and whispered, "We're going to save your baby, princess of the House of Smoke," he said with a rough voice. "But you have to lie back, no matter the pain. Do you understand?" Leonidas's hands trembled a little as they held her arm and gently urged her back.

Slowly, slowly, the keening sound coming out of her mouth diminished, and she eased back into the water.

Lucian shook with relief and the emotional overload that gripped him.

Arabella panted, her breath heaving in and out. Her beautiful face twisted with a pain that Lucian almost couldn't look upon. Between gasps, she called to him. "Lucian."

He bent back down to her. "I'm here."

"I told…" More panting. "The baby." She swallowed and seemed to deliberately deepen her breaths. "I told him… you would come."

Holy mother of magic, he prayed, *please don't let me lose her. Please.*

"Of course, I came," Lucian whispered. "You are everything to me."

Arabella nodded, jerkily, splashing the water around her face and up onto her cheek. She was nearly submerged. "We have to make it." Her voice was so soft, it was like she was talking to herself. Or to the baby. "For Daddy."

Lucian couldn't breathe. She was holding his entire life in those words.

Then Arabella gritted her teeth and breathed through them in short bursts—in and out, in and out—and a scream welled up from so deep inside her that it sounded like it was turning her inside out. She writhed in the water, clenching and bearing down. She flailed her hand at Rachel, grabbing hold of her shirt, fisting it, and dragging her closer. "The baby… is coming…" Arabella gasped out.

"Holy shit!" Rachel looked down at Arabella's belly. "Lucian, her clothes!"

What the hell?

"Oh, for fuck's sake, Lucian!" Rachel cried. "Do your magic thing and get rid of her clothes!"

He just blinked for a moment and then realized… *the baby was coming.*

Lucian hastily lifted a hand and flicked away Arabella's clothes, replacing them with a gown that would give his mate some privacy from the three men hovering over her, keeping her alive during the birth of his son.

"Rachel… can you…" Lucian nodded helplessly at his mate, his hands busy with pumping healing magic in her.

"Oh God!" The woman looked completely startled and terrified, but she jumped to her feet and ran around the back of Cinaed to the end of the tub. Once there, she thrust her hands into the water and underneath Arabella's gown.

Arabella lurched up out of the water, screaming, only, this time, he could see the writhing of her belly as his son moved, preparing for his arrival.

"Oh my God! Oh my God! I see his head!" Rachel yelled.

Lucian turned away from the panic on her face and focused on Arabella's. Her eyes were squeezed tight, her teeth were clenched hard, and she was pushing, pushing, pushing... Lucian flushed every bit of magic he had left through his hands and into her, giving her every bit of borrowed strength he could.

"It's happening! He's coming!" Rachel's voice hiked up hysterically.

Arabella groaned and pushed, and in a moment of undefined quiet, only the sloshing of water and scrambling for movement... *his son was born.* He knew it by the gasping look of relief on Arabella's beautiful face. He couldn't tear his eyes from her shining green eyes, not until he heard...

The baby's cry.

His head whipped to the sound of its own volition. Rachel's eyes were wide as saucers, but she was cradling his newborn son in the water, holding his head above it and letting his little body—an impossibly tiny body—float next to his mother's legs. His son's hands were fisted up tight to his chin, legs tucked against his small belly, but his eyes were wide and wondering. *Green eyes.* Just like his mother. And the small cry that had announced his entrance into the world had subsided into a tiny pout that worked soundlessly.

Lucian was the same—his mouth opened and closed, but no sound came out.

"Let me see him," Arabella said, her words half sob.

Lucian was whipped out of his shock. "Arabella, my love." He stared in wonder as she sat up in the bath. "Are you…"

His brothers had already released her. They were grinning like fools next to the bath, just like Cinaed, all as wordless as he, but they couldn't possibly have half his joy.

"I'm fine," Arabella said, still breathless. She was radiant.

His hands held her up, touching her skin in wonder—the fire was gone from her body.

She nodded to affirm it again. "I'm okay, Lucian." She held her hands out to Rachel. "I want my son."

Rachel looked uncertain how to move the baby from the water to his mother's waiting arms. Cinaed leaned down and gently supported the baby with her. A look passed between them, and Cinaed's wide grin seemed to leap across the air and infect Rachel. By the time the two of them brought the baby to Arabella's arms for her to cradle against her drenched gown, Rachel and Cinaed were side by side, leaning into each other. Once they gave the baby over, Cinaed's arm slipped around Rachel's shoulders, and he held her tight to his side.

Lucian's brothers each clapped a hand to one of his shoulders. Leonidas still looked gray, but his smile was nearly breaking his face. Leksander had tears in his eyes that he seemed determined not to let fall. By his side, Erelah leaned back, looking on with the same wonder that was bursting from Lucian's heart.

But his tears were burned off by a fiery joy that radiated inside him like the sun. He reached a tremulous hand to his son's head. Arabella was already snuggling him to her chest like a pro.

"You did it." He breathed out the words, amazed. *This woman…* how had he managed to keep this amazing woman?

"*We* did it." She beamed up at him. *Those green eyes…* just like their son. The precious new life that fixed everything—Lucian could feel the holes in his heart healing, the poison banishing, the fear, anxiety, and sheer terror at the thought of losing them both evaporating into mist. The blessing of his son's birth renewed Lucian's life in an intensely magical way.

"He needs a name," Arabella said, her grin catching up to everyone else's.

Lucian's face was still locked up in wonder. In all the worries leading up to this moment, he had never truly believed it would happen. Not until his son appeared before his eyes, blinking up at him and nuzzling his mother. Choosing a name seemed like inviting the fates to curse him once again.

But they hadn't.

And then it hit Lucian in the chest, a bittersweet feeling that fit just right. "He shall be named Larik. Larik Smoke, dragon prince of the House of Smoke."

Arabella's smile dimmed a little. "Your father's name?"

Of course, she couldn't know. Not yet. He would tell her, but later. "Yes." He snuck a look to Leksander. His brother gave him a short nod. Before he could catch Leonidas's eye, his brother gripped his shoulder, gave it a squeeze, and then turned away, head bent. Leksander went after him, gesturing Erelah to follow.

Lucian turned back to find Cinaed and Rachel had likewise stepped back from the tub. Only they weren't slipping away—they were locked in an embrace that burned with enough heat to set the forest on fire.

Finally, Lucian's smile arrived on his face.

Arabella saw them as well and grinned up at him. "Maybe we'll have another dragonling in the House of Smoke soon."

"Shhh!" he said, returning her grin and bending close to his beautiful mate and his precious newborn son. "You'll put a hex on it, if you speak of it too soon."

She put a hand to his cheek, and he was so relieved to find it the same temperature as his. "It's never too early to speak of love."

"You're right. As usual." He brushed a soft kiss across the top of his son's head. Then he leaned in to kiss Arabella's cheek. "I promise never to argue with you again."

She laughed, and the water sloshed around her. "Liar."

He grinned. "Yes, probably so." Then he kissed her and decided that this moment would never be topped in all the next five hundred years.

Chapter Eighteen

In less than twenty-four hours, Arabella was already recovered from the most horrible and wonderful day of her life—the day she became a mom.

She glanced over her shoulder at little Larik. He was wrapped up in a magic-conjured blanket more soft than any human-made material and cuddled up in the crook of his grandmother's arm. The queen was now the Queen Mother, and while the throne room was filled with the hundred or so dragons of the House, the Queen Mother only had eyes for the tiniest dragon in the room. Arabella didn't blame her a bit—she could hardly take her eyes off the baby herself—but Arabella knew the sad, sweet smile that lit the graceful Queen Mother's face was heartbreak mixed with love. The woman had lost her mate and gained a grandson all in one day. And who knew how long the House of Smoke would have its Queen Mother?

Because of that, Arabella fought her natural urge to want Larik in her arms at all times and let the Queen Mother have him whenever she asked. Even Lucian gave the baby over to his mother whenever he caught her gazing at him wistfully. And now that they were back in the throne room, gathered for the coronation, it was the perfect time for grandma to soothe little Larik's tiny baby protests. For being so fearsome in the womb, he was practically an angel now that he was born. Although she wasn't sure *angel* was the right word, now that Arabella knew *actual* angels—they'd helped bring Larik into the world, but they were much more fierce and strange than her beautiful, perfect, sweet-tempered infant son.

She was just a little bit in love. But then he was Lucian's baby—how could she not love him?

Arabella turned her gaze back to the gorgeous, gentle man who was her mate, the father of her son… and now, the king of the House of Smoke. His gaze roamed the assembled dragons, down in number by the twenty they lost to the poison. Tytus had been killed, and his demon mercenaries either killed or fled, but the three brothers working together, using all their fae magic, hadn't been fast enough to save all of those who had been taken down by the dragon-talon-tipped darts and their magical poison. Some had been hit ten or twenty times and were dead before the brothers could even reach them. Some had hung on for longer, but eventually the poison took them. Leonidas and Leksander had left members of their House suffering in order to chase after her and her son. Baby Larik owed them his life... and Leonidas was still paying the price for it. He hadn't passed away in the night, like so many of the House of Smoke had, and most of the gray pallor had disappeared from his face, but he still appeared drawn and worn.

Lucian told her the poison had nearly brought Leonidas to his wyvern form. They had almost lost him. It made Arabella cry every time she thought of it.

But now he was weaving through the crowd, smiling and clasping hands with the other dragons of the House. Leksander followed behind him, doing the same. They were both working their way toward the front where Lucian was sitting on the throne next to hers.

Queen Arabella. She was pretty sure she would *never* get used to that.

Lucian caught her staring at the way he filled out his royal tunic with the golden dragon magically emblazoned on the chest. He wore a golden cape, so light the tips floated in the breeze, and a thin circle of gold rested on his head, newly crowned. She had one as well, although her dress looked more like the mating gown she wore just six weeks ago when she agreed to risk her life and her heart to belong to the crown prince of the House of Smoke. The white filmy tendrils of it floated in the same unseen breeze.

Lucian smiled. "I know what you're thinking, Arabella Sharp."

"Do you?" she asked with a smirk. "I thought mindreading only happened in dragon form."

"I don't have to be a mindreader to recognize that look in your eye."

"The one that says *I can't believe I'm sitting on this throne?*"

He lowered his voice and leaned over the arm of his ornately carved throne chair. "The one that says you can't wait to come in my bed."

"Lucian!" She darted a look at the crowd, but if they heard, no one gave notice. "What about the baby?" Although the truth was that her body had already recovered from the near-death experience of giving birth to her dragonling son—the healing power of dragon magic was breathtaking—but with all the turmoil and House matters to be settled and attending to baby Larik, there hadn't been even a moment of time for her to reconnect with her mate. And she had a powerful, almost overwhelming, urge to do just that—to feel Lucian's arms around her, to revel in his kisses and his lovemaking. *They had made it.* She had lived. She had given him a son. And now she had five hundred years to enjoy every inch of his gorgeous, manly form, worry-free.

He winked. "The baby will have to find his own mate. But he has a few hundred years in which to do so."

She had to bite her lip to hold back the grin. "How soon is this party over?"

He dropped his gaze to her ample breasts—they had grown at least a size, maybe two, since the birth, swelling with magical baby milk to feed her new dragonling. "Not soon enough for me," he said, his voice full of sexual promise.

Arabella squirmed with the heat gushing to her

core. It really couldn't be right for her to be hot for her mate in the middle of a coronation ceremony—but she couldn't help herself. Not with Lucian looking at her that way.

A small commotion at the end of the long throne room made Arabella's heart seize—

But it was only Cinaed and Rachel finally making their entrance.

They checked their hurried pace as they stumbled through the door and all eyes were suddenly on them. Cinaed straightened his long coat—that ancient formal style like Lucian's, only less royal and minus the golden cape—and Rachel fluttered her hands over the magical dress someone had conjured for her. It was flame-red and emphasized all her curves. She seemed flustered by the sudden attention. Cinaed took her hand and led her down the center aisle. A wave of head-turns and smirks followed them.

Arabella narrowed her eyes, scrutinizing her best friend as she marched down the room toward the throne. "Do you think they..." She flicked a look to Lucian.

His smirk was halfway to a laugh. "Every dragon in the room can smell the sex on them."

Oh, gawd. "Keep that to yourself!" she hissed. Rachel would be mortified.

Lucian gave her a quizzical look. "I thought you blessed their—"

"Shh!" she said as they grew close enough to hear. *Yes,* she wanted Rachel and Cinaed to get together. She hoped they'd spent the last twenty-four hours christening every square inch of the guest apartment. Or Cinaed's lair. Or the elevator for all she cared. She just didn't want her best friend to be embarrassed in any way about anything. The romance between them was fresh and new and... Arabella didn't want it adversely influenced by anything. Not until it had a chance to take root and flower.

Cinaed guided Rachel to the left side of the dais where the two thrones—Arabella's and Lucian's—stood, along with the Queen Mother's seat to the back. On the right, Leksander and Leonidas stood in a similar spot. Now that everyone had arrived, Arabella guessed the ceremony could begin. Rachel continued to fuss and tug at her dress as if the fit on it was almost too tight. Arabella fought off the grin that came with that thought—she was sure Cinaed had conjured it to his own liking. He and Lucian exchanged brief nods. Arabella wondered what exactly that was about, but both dragons seemed pleased with whatever it meant.

Lucian stood and raised his arms to quiet the stray murmurs still going around the room. "Dragons of the House of Smoke, a great tragedy has visited our House." A hush fell over the crowd. "And a great blessing. We have a new prince…" He swept his hand out and smiled at his mother, who barely looked up from her doting on little Larik. The crowd roared its approval, clapping and stamping their feet. When it settled a little, Lucian added, "And a new queen…" More roaring approval, and Lucian beckoned her to stand. She was more than capable—her legs were strong under her, and the rest of her was quickly forgetting that she'd almost been consumed in a magical fire from the inside out less than twenty-four hours before— but somehow the adoration that was coming in waves made her a little weak behind the knees. All she'd done was love their prince, now king, as they did. But she understood that it was precisely that True Love which had made everything possible.

When the cheering slowed, Lucian finally gave her a nod that let her sit again.

He faced them. "And we have a new king," he said solemnly. "My father was a great man with a good and wise heart. My son will never know him, and our House has a hole in it where his strength used to live." There was silence a moment as Lucian seemed to struggle for words.

Arabella clenched the arms of her throne. Her heart hurt for him. She didn't think there would ever be a time when she wouldn't want to ease any pain he felt, kiss away any sorrow, any darkness that might loom.

Lucian swallowed and continued. "We lost many good dragons in the last twenty-four hours. Friends. Brothers. Some who leave mates and dragonlings behind. They will always have a home with us, as our own blood, under our care." A murmur of approval went up with heads nodding all around. "There is much I do not understand about how this attack was able to penetrate our defenses. I promise you, we will get to the root of this demon infestation and all that it means. But in the meantime, I've ordered additional security measures and armaments put in place. We have known peace for so long, my friends, so long... but there are things afoot in the magical world, and it is a dangerous time. The Summer Queen warned me, but I didn't take her meaning at the time. I'm still not sure I do. But my son..." He waved a hand back to Larik and the Queen Mother. "My son secures the treaty for another generation—"

Lucian was cut off by Leksander speaking into his phone. *"What?"* Leksander's gaze locked with Lucian's, eyes wide. "Zephan's at the perimeter. He's seeking an audience."

"You have got to be fucking kidding—"

"He's saying he's the representative of the Winter Court, and he's here to witness the birth. That we're *advised* not to deny him." Leksander scowled, but that had nothing on the panic raging through Arabella's body.

She jolted up out of her throne chair. "Lucian, *no.*"

But he was just shaking his head. "The treaty protects Larik, just as it protects any prince of the House of Smoke."

"That didn't stop Tytus from nearly killing all of us!" Tears threatened her eyes. She flicked a look to the Queen Mother holding her baby, just to reassure herself they were okay. Lucian's mother was still seated, but her eyes were set hard.

"I don't have any direct evidence tying Tytus's attack to Zephan…"

"Lucian!" She couldn't believe he would even consider letting that monster into the keep.

Lucian held up his hands. "I'm sure Zephan was involved in some way. I *will* find out how. But for now, Arabella... there are formalities that keep the peace and fae representatives giving official witness to the birth of the new dragon prince is one of them."

She just kept shaking her head. Then she left the throne to hustle back to the Queen Mother's side. Arabella took her baby back in her arms and held him tight. The Queen Mother rose and stood tall, facing Lucian.

"You have to allow it, Lucian," she said, and there was no question in her voice.

Lucian grimaced and looked back to Leksander.

"I can't see a way around it, either," he said with a scowl.

They both looked to Leonidas, but he just shrugged.

Lucian hesitated for a long moment, then he nodded to his brothers. "Protect the prince." They hustled over to stand on either side of Arabella and Larik and the Queen Mother. Cinaed left Rachel at the side of the throne dais and took a protective stance in front of all of them.

The entire throne room tensed as Lucian lifted his chin to Leksander.

He spoke into the phone. "Let him in."

Barely a second passed before Zephan appeared at the back of the throne room, obviously using his fae magic to get inside the keep once the wards were down. Heads jerked his way, and a dozen dragons shifted, hyper-vigilant, but they stayed in place. Arabella clutched her baby with both hands as her heart hammered. The Queen Mother moved in front of Arabella and Larik, then shifted and reared up, the full splendor of her golden wings unfurling in front of Arabella and the baby, blocking her view but protecting them.

"Well, there's no need for panic, House of Smoke," Zephan said in a casual, droll way that made Arabella's stomach clench. His voice drew closer as he spoke. Arabella peeked around the Queen Mother's wings to see him approaching Lucian at his throne. "And I told you before, Lucian Smoke of the House of Smoke... I wished to be notified when the birth of your dragonling was imminent. As you know, it has to be witnessed to be official."

"Fuck off, Zephan. You sent Tytus to kill my mate and my son." Lucian's hands had shifted, and his talons flexed. Several dragons in the crowd edged forward.

Zephan looked offended. "I cannot be held responsible for the actions of some random dragon."

"He said you were creating demons. Infecting humans—"

"I'm not infecting humans with anything!" Zephan's voice boomed and vibrated the walls of the throne room. Then he calmed and gave a grim smile. "Take care with your accusations, dragon king. Humans are vile creatures quite capable of their own evil."

Arabella didn't believe a word he was saying—supposedly the fae couldn't lie, but what did that even mean? Zephan was as tricky as they came.

The fae prince let out an elaborate sigh. "Besides, that's not your biggest problem, King Lucian of the House of Smoke. You have yet to fulfill the treaty."

Lucian hesitated, and even from the side of the throne dais and behind his mother's protective golden wings, Arabella could see his teeth grinding. But he turned and gestured to Arabella. "Show him," he said, tersely.

His mother hesitated, but then shifted back to human, revealing Arabella standing behind her with the baby. Larik made a small sound, a tiny cry, and nuzzled closer against her chest. She held him tight. If Zephan even made a move toward them…

But he didn't.

Instead, he just shrugged. "Oh yes, I know about the dragonling. I'm sure he's a fine, strapping little monster. But his birth is far from sufficient to fulfill the treaty."

"What the hell are you talking about?" Lucian demanded.

Zephan held his hands up like he was innocent, but Arabella knew better. She didn't know how, but she *knew* Zephan was orchestrating something here. Something awful.

Her stomach clenched as an evil smile snuck on Zephan's face.

He turned to face the Queen Mother. "Do you recall the controversy, Alexis? When you were first mated to the dearly-departed Larik the Elder? As I recall, you were a dragon mating to another dragon, something that was unprecedented. There was much wagering in the Winter Court as to whether that alone would break the treaty."

"The treaty held," Lucian's mother said, stiffly.

Zephan tilted his head, but the smile was growing into a smirk. "Indeed it did. Your love was True, and we all felt it ripple across magical space, didn't we?" His eyes glittered. "And then the triplets came, and that was the final reassurance, wasn't it?" He looked at them each by turns—Arabella, Leonidas, Leksander, Lucian, and then finally the Queen Mother. "Did you feel it again, Alexis? Just yesterday, when little Larik was born? Or were you too mired in the tragic loss of your mate?"

The Queen Mother went rigid, not moving or speaking... but Lucian's eyes were wide and questioning. Arabella didn't understand it either.

Zephan's smirk just grew. "You thought it was a blessing when three sons were given to you, but I knew better. I knew your time was coming to an end."

Arabella's heart lurched. *"Lucian."* She begged with her eyes for an explanation, but he just shook his head, looking as confused as she was.

An awkward moment reigned. "Mother, what is he talking about?" Lucian finally asked.

The Queen Mother didn't answer at first. Then she took a step forward. Then another. Until she was close to the front of the throne dais, looking down at Zephan as he smirked up at her.

"When my sons were born," she said loud enough for the entire hall to hear. There was a horrible dread in her voice, but her eyes were locked onto Zephan's face. "The entire world felt it." She dragged her gaze from Zephan to meet Lucian's wide-eyed stare. "We *felt* it, Lucian."

Lucian's face went slack.

Felt what? Arabella wanted to scream. But she was clutching her baby and holding onto the hope that all this was one big misunderstanding. That everything she had been through hadn't been for *nothing.*

"Of course, you did," Zephan purred. "That magical shock occurs every time the treaty is renewed. An echo through magical space of the power of the first treaty, forged in the powerful magic of death and True Love. That's how we knew, Alexis. That was the ultimate proof that your dragon-dragon coupling had fulfilled the requirements of the treaty when your three boys were born. But you didn't feel it this time, did you?"

A heartbeat. Then two. *"No,"* came her whispered reply. Then she slowly turned away from Lucian and looked back with tears in her eyes to her other two sons, standing next to Arabella and the baby—Leonidas and Leksander.

"But... but I'm the *prototokos,*" Lucian protested. "The first-born—"

"Do you really think that *when* you exited the

womb has any real significance?" Zephan sneered. "You are all three the product of the True Love pairing. All three of you survived the birthing. But in your arrogance, you presumed to know magic of which you are barely aware."

Breath was held all around the throne room.

"All three dragon princes of the House of Smoke must produce dragonlings through a True Love pairing or the treaty *will* be broken." The triumph on Zephan's face struck horror through Arabella's chest.

No... She looked to Leonidas. *"The curse,"* she whispered.

Leonidas briefly closed his eyes, the gray pallor returning to his face.

Leksander was likewise pale.

The horror on Lucian's face struck her through the chest.

The tiny, innocent baby in her arms *wasn't enough...* they had made it through, all of them, but the toll it had taken... and now two more princes of the House of Smoke had to bring dragonlings into the world in order to save it. Leonidas, who was cursed to turn wyvern if he ever fell in love and who had already nearly been turned by the poison. Leksander, who was in love with an angeling who would never return it. Both had to win the True Love of a human woman or not only would their lives end... but a twelve-thousand-year-old treaty as well.

Arabella let her tears fall freely and drip down onto her sweet baby's face.

Leonidas's story continues in…

CHOSEN BY A DRAGON

(Fallen Immortals 4)

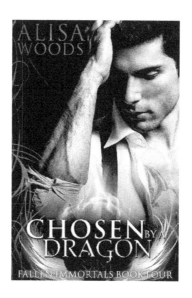

Grab Chosen by a Dragon today!

Subscribe to Alisa's newsletter

for new releases and giveaways

http://smarturl.it/AWsubscribeBARDS

About the Author

Alisa Woods lives in the Midwest with her husband and family, but her heart will always belong to the beaches and mountains where she grew up. She writes sexy paranormal romances about complicated men and the strong women who love them. Her books explore the struggles we all have, where we resist—and succumb to—our most tempting vices as well as our greatest desires. No matter the challenge, Alisa firmly believes that hearts can mend and love will triumph over all.

www.AlisaWoodsAuthor.com

Made in the USA
Las Vegas, NV
10 October 2021